ALSO BY ELIZABETH BERG

FAMILY TRADITIONS:
Celebrations for Holidays and Everyday

DURABLE GOODS

TALK BEFORE SLEEP

TALK
BEFORE SLEEP

A NOVEL

Elizabeth Berg

Random House New York

Library of Congress Cataloging-in-Publication Data
Berg, Elizabeth.
Talk before sleep / Elizabeth Berg. — 1st ed.
p.   cm.
1. Cancer—Patients—United States—Fiction.   2. Friendship—
United States—Fiction.   3. Women—United States—Fiction.
I. Title.
PS3552.E6996T35   1994
813'.54—dc20   93-47443

Manufactured in the United States of America on acid-free paper
98765432
First Edition

Book design by Oksana Kushnir

For women with cancer
who have found their fire,
and for those who are
still searching.

Not long ago, I lost a very important friend to breast cancer. I wanted to write about my experience in a fictional way, to create characters and events that, although imagined, would testify to the emotional truth of all that happened. My purpose was twofold: I wanted to demonstrate the strength and salvation of women's friendships; and I wanted to personalize the devastating effects of losing someone to this disease, which continues to claim lives daily. It is important to say that this is a work of fiction and both the characters and the events in the novel are products of my imagination. The only truth is that the fight against breast cancer has gone on for too many for too long; and the burden is on all of us to change that.

If we look at the path, we do not
see the sky. We are earth people
on a spiritual journey to the stars.
Our quest, our earth walk, is to look
within, to know who we are, to see that
we are connected to all things,
that there is no separation,
only in the mind.

—Native American, source unknown

TALK BEFORE SLEEP

This morning, before I came to Ruth's house, I
made yet another casserole for my husband and
my daughter. Meggie likes casseroles while Joe
only endures them, but they are all I can manage right
now. I put the dish in the refrigerator, with a note taped
on it telling how long to cook it, and at what tempera-
ture, and that they should have a salad, too.

Next I did a little laundry—washed Meggie's favorite skirt, then laid it on top of the dryer and pressed
the pleats in with the flat of my hand. I love doing this
because I love the smell of laundry soap and the memory
it brings of lying outside on warm days, watching my
mother peg huge white bedsheets onto the clothesline.
Those sheets glowed with the light blue color white
clothes radiate when they are extremely clean. My
mother seemed to be fighting with them sometimes,
muttering at them as best she could through the wooden
clothespins she held in her mouth, insisting that they
stay anchored in one place while they pulled and yanked
to be free, their wet snapping sounds a protest. I always
thought maybe we should let them go. Maybe they had a
mission. Maybe the sheets were really people who had
started all over again, come back on some low rung and
now were ready to fly up to heaven for a promotion—
say to a paramecium. I viewed all things on the earth as
equal, in terms of the Grand Scheme. Vice presidents
and river rocks had nothing up on each other. So the
cotton fibers of a bedsheet could easily return as a sim-

4   ple form of water life, or, for that matter, as a movie
star who drove white motorcycles through the glamor-
ous hills of Hollywood.

I also like doing laundry for the feeling of connection it brings me, especially now, when I see my family
too little, when most of my time is taken up with things
they have no part of. With my hand on Meggie's skirt, I
can see her small, keyhole-shaped knees, the sliding-
down socks she wears, the nearly worn-out sneakers she
won't let me replace. I see her schoolgirl blouses and
the half-heart necklace she likes to wear every day
lately, advertising the fact that she is someone's best
friend. And then, saving the best for last, I see her face,
her still slightly rounded cheeks, her stick-out ears, her
gorgeous red hair and matching freckles. She has just
learned to make her own ponytail, and she stands softly
grunting at the mirror in the morning until the lumps
are gone—or nearly so. I can't attend to these small
things now—sometimes I sleep at Ruth's and am not
there in the morning and Meggie goes to school with
messy hair; and with questionable color combinations,
no doubt. She's lucky she's only nine; it doesn't really
matter yet. Her bangs need cutting, her toenails too,
probably—Joe can't keep up with these everyday details and still work the number of hours he's required
to. I know that eventually all will return to normal at
my house, and then we will feel better—and worse,
too, of course.

For now, I roll out piecrust, let myself be soothed
by the sound of low-voiced interviews or oldies on the
radio. I have learned so much lately about the salvation

to be found in caretaking, whatever form that caring takes.

Today, while I was rushing around the kitchen making dinner at seven-thirty in the morning, Meggie asked, "Is Ruth your only best friend?"

"Yes," I said, surprised at the evenness of my tone.

"Oh." She sighed softly. "I'm sorry for you, Mommy."

"I know you are."

"Was she always your best friend?"

"No."

"Did you have one before her?"

"I guess so," I told her, then sent her off to school. And then I thought about Carol Conroy. The first time I made a promise with my whole heart, it was to Carol Conroy, and it required me to take care of her rabbit, Ecclesiastes. Carol, who liked very much the sound of words she found in the Bible, was leaving our small New England town to visit Disneyland for ten entire days. My jealousy was mitigated somewhat by the importance of the task she had assigned me. "You have to feed this rabbit and change his water every day," Carol told me solemnly. "And on every *third* day, you have to clean up his poops. It's not too bad unless he gets sick. But you have to do it even if he gets sick! Now, promise." I stood up straight and promised with my whole heart—I could feel it straining with earnestness—because I loved Carol Conroy in the way that ten-year-old girls do love each other, with a fierce,

6   raggedy flame destined to go out. I vowed to do everything she said unless I died.

Ecclesiastes did get sick—maybe because of some
licorice I fed him—and I ended up having to clean his
cage several times a day for four days straight. The rabbit's illness only endeared him to me. I didn't resent
him; I wanted to help him; and I felt gilded when he
recovered. Years later, I would say it was Ecclesiastes
that prompted me to become a nurse. And now, years
after becoming a nurse—in fact, years after having left
the profession to take care of my family, I have again
made a promise with my whole heart, again out of love
for my best friend. Only this time my friend's name is
Ruth. And this time the flame is steady, in no danger of
going out. I would say it is of the eternal variety.

S o now it is ten-thirty in the morning, and Ruth is
in the bathtub, and I am straightening out her bed.
She has a white eyelet dust ruffle, white sheets
with eyelet trim, a blue-and-white striped comforter,
Laura Ashley. There are four fat goosedown pillows,
each covered with beautiful embroidered pillowcases,
white on white. There is a stack of magazines piled high
on the floor and a collection of crystals on the bedside
table: rose quartz, amethyst, and a clear white one with
a delicate, fractured pattern running through it. They
are not working. She is dying, though we don't know
when. We are waiting. She is only forty-three and I am

only forty-two and all this will not stop being surprising.

I hear her calling my name and I crack open the bathroom door. "Yes?"

"Could you come in here?" Her voice is a little shaky and I realize this is the first time I have heard her sound afraid.

I sit on the floor beside her, rest my arms along the edge of the tub to lean in close, though what I am thinking is that I ought to get in with her. She has used bubble bath and the sweet smell rises up warm and nearly palpable between us. Tahitian Ginger. The label on the bottle features happy natives who do not believe in Western medicine. The bubbles have mostly disappeared; I can see the outline of her body in the water. She is half swimming, turning slightly side to side, hips rising languidly up and down. Her breasts are gone.

"What's up?" I say.

She squeezes her bath sponge over her head. She is almost bald, but not quite. Dark strands of hair cling to the bottom of her head and her neck. Duck fluff, we call it. I told her to shave her head and she'd look great, like a movie star, like a rock singer. It's the latest rage, I told her. "Nah," she said. "What's left, I want to keep. It has sentimental value."

"I was wondering what happens when I die," she says now. "I was thinking, how are they sure? Are they really sure? I mean, what if I get buried alive?"

"They're sure," I tell her. "You sort of . . . shut down. Your heart stops, and your breathing. Certain reflexes disappear, you know, like the pupils in your eyes

8   don't react." She watches me, holding absolutely still, looking like a colorized sculpture of herself. I sigh, then add, "And you get cold, you get real cold, okay? Your skin doesn't feel warm anymore. They're absolutely sure."

"Oh," she says. "Okay. Just checking." She is relieved; you can see it in the uncreasing of her forehead, in the loosening to normal of the area around her mouth. "Wash my back, will you?"

She sits up and rests her forehead on her raised knees. I bump the washcloth over newly revealed bones, the delicate scapulas, the orderly line of vertebrae. "I'm becoming exoskeletal," she says, her voice muffled. "I'm turning into a lobster. Maybe when we die we go back incrementally. You know, a little to the sea, then on to the heavens." She thinks a moment, then says, "I was just lying in here and I felt kind of tired and . . . weird, and then I thought, wait—is this it? I mean, how will I know?" She leans back, frowns. "Is that the same question I just asked? Am I making any sense? Do I keep asking the same goddamn question?"

I'd been making dinner. I had The Oprah Winfrey Show *on the little kitchen TV. The phone rang and I wiped my hands on my apron and answered it and she said, "It's in my brain."*

"No," I say, "it's not the same question. It's different. First you wanted to know how *they'd* know; now you want to know how *you'll* know. Different question entirely. You will know, though. You won't be the same person you are now when it happens. You'll be, I don't know . . . wiser."

"Okay." She stands up, asks for a towel, tells me she's done.

"I should think so," I say. "You've been in there for an hour."

"Have I? Jesus, I thought it was about five minutes."

"That's okay. I was having a good time waiting for you. I was reading your diary."

"Find anything good?"

"The sex stuff. That's good. But it's all bullshit."

"You wish."

I help her into a nightgown: white, white-lace trim, thin strands of ribbon hanging down the front.

She climbs in bed, pulls the covers up. She is tired, so pale. But her blue eyes are still beautiful and her face such a perfect shape you could walk into the room and see her and first just be jealous.

"I suppose it could be tonight, couldn't it?" she says. "God, it really could."

I was with her, sitting in the corner of the examining room, while she read questions off her list. She was pushing to know exactly how and when. She's that way: if she'd ever had to go to confession, she'd have torn down the curtain separating her and the priest. "Hey! Look at me when I'm talking to you," she would have told him.

Her oncologist was wearing a blue suit, a white shirt, a beautiful Italian silk tie and a gold Rolex watch. He was handsome and very sad, leaning up against the little sink in the room with his arms crossed over his chest and one leg crossed over the other, too. Obviously, this was too much for him. I think when he first met Ruth he fell in love with her and, guiltless, stayed there—though at an antiseptic distance Ruth re-

10   *gretted. Falling in love with her was a liability that came with being a man around her. Finally, he said, "All right, yes. It could be any time. Depending on how it happens. If it's from brain metastasis, it could be at any time."*

Of course she has other options. Respiratory failure, say, from lung metastasis. Liver failure from the metastasis there. Think of those cartoons where people are run over by steamrollers and then get up and walk around. You'll be seeing Ruth. She put a new message on her answering machine the other day—she thought the old one sounded too sad. I stood behind her and watched her do it, her back so straight. The only thing that revealed what was really happening is that one of her feet rapidly tapped the floor the whole time she was talking. "It's me," she said. "I can't come to the phone right now. But leave me a message and probably you should make it a good one, okay? Okay, 'bye." She says "okay" all the time, Ruth. Before, we'd be making plans to go somewhere. "Okay, okay, so I'll meet you there at seven, okay?" she'd say.

"Will you stay here tonight?" she asks now.

"Of course." I hope my face doesn't reflect any of the ambivalence I feel. Another night away. I haven't paid bills. I need to call my mother. Joe and I haven't had sex in over six weeks. I feel sometimes as if I'm opening a too-full closet and shoving something else in, then leaning against the door so it won't burst open.

Later, when she is asleep, I'll call home. "Please understand," I'll say.

Ruth pats the bed. "Here, take a load off. Should we watch a movie?"

I stretch out beside her. "I'd rather talk."

"Okay," she says. "But mostly you. I get too short of breath. It's getting worse. Have you noticed?"

"Yes."

She nods. "Yeah."

"What should I talk about?" I ask.

"Me," she says. "Tell me a story about me. If I seem to fall asleep, make sure I'm not dead. I think you have to call somebody if I am, right?"

"Right. The coroner."

"Yes. And call Michael, too. You be the one to tell him. I don't want his father to. He'll fuck it up. But if I'm just sleeping, don't get offended, okay?"

"Okay," I say. "All right: the story of Ruth. So to speak. Well, the first time I saw you, you really pissed me off."

"You were jealous," she says.

"I know," I say. "Everybody was. But also you were being a pain in the ass."

"Exactly wrong," she says. "You're projecting again."

"Exactly right," I agree.

I don't like parties. I hate parties. They make me nervous and irritable and slightly nauseated. And they make me feel exposed in a terrible way, as if I'm walking around with the back of my dress missing and everybody knows but me. But of course I go to parties. You have to, sometimes, the way you have to go to the dentist. At a party is where I met Ruth.

12   She was sitting in a corner of the living room, surrounded by people, and she was saying things that were making them laugh. She was irritatingly beautiful: raven-haired, blue-eyed, neatly petite. She had perfect teeth and she was wearing expensive-looking boots with a gorgeous blue skirt and sweater. I'd heard about her, about how talented an artist she was, how interesting, how much fun. "I hate that woman," I told my husband, pointing in her direction.

"Who's that?" he asked.

"Ruth Thomas. Can't stand her."

"How do you know her?"

"I don't. But I know about her. Can't stand her."

"So don't talk to her," he said, and I said fine, I wouldn't. But when I went into the tiny downstairs bathroom to hide, she came bursting in the door.

"Oh, sorry!" she said, and started to leave. But then, seeing that I was sitting, legs crossed, on the closed lid of the toilet, drinking my martini, she stopped. "Are you—have you finished?"

"Finished what?"

"Do you need the toilet?"

"I'm sitting here," I said.

"Yes, I can see that. However, you can sit a lot of places. Whereas someone who has to take a piss needs to sit right here, okay?"

I got up, started to squeeze past her. "You can have it back when I'm done," she said. "This is the best place at this party."

I waited outside, finished my drink. I heard a flush, then her voice saying, "You can come in now." I waited for her to exit and when she didn't, I went in with her. She was washing her face at the sink, splashing cold water on herself. Obviously she didn't worry about her mascara smearing. When she looked up, I saw why: she wasn't wearing any. It wasn't a good political statement, though, because she didn't need any. "Hand me that towel, will you?" she asked, and I gave her a paper guest towel. "I hate these things," she said. "Makes you feel they believe their guests are diseased."

I shrugged. I was warming up to her a little. I'm afraid I like critical people when they rag on others because it makes me feel exonerated.

She threw the towel away, looked at it lying in the white wicker trash basket. "Jesus," she said. "Little pink hearts!"

I extended my hand. "Ann Stanley."

She shook it firmly. "Ruth Thomas."

I held up my empty glass. "Would you like a martini?"

"I'll mix, okay?" she said. "No one can make them like I do."

I leaned against the kitchen counter, watching her while she made our drinks. She had a flask in her purse, a lovely silver thing filled with gin. "Where'd you get that?" I asked.

"A Christmas present from my husband," she said. She nodded in the general direction of the living room. She wasn't wearing a wedding ring. "It was an attempt to bring us closer. See, we can now, at a moment's notice, get drunk together. Isn't that romantic?"

We sat at the kitchen table and got through the what-brings-you-here material. And then it was on to

14 movies. She asked if I'd seen *Sophie's Choice* and I said no and she said I should, it was terrific, ripped your heart out and flung it onto the floor. "I'll go with you and see it again," she said. "You should see it with a woman."

My husband came into the kitchen, looked at me sitting there with Ruth. I gave him a slight raise of eyebrow, a tiny defensive shrug. He sat down and introduced himself, then had the good sense to leave.

"All right, how long have *you* been married?" she asked, sighing, and I knew we had a lot to talk about. I could forgive her good looks. She was capable of a scary kind of honesty I was ready for, although until that moment, I hadn't realized how much I'd been needing to meet someone I might be able to say everything to.

She is sleeping. I do make sure, of course. I watch for the rise and fall of the sheet over her. You must stop your own breathing to do this. Otherwise, you count your own movements as that of the person you're watching. You also must never check for a person's pulse using your thumb, or you'll feel your own heartbeat. Actually, I plan on doing that if I'm the one who's here when Ruth dies. I plan on giving her my heartbeat before I let her go.

I move off the bed slowly, tiptoe into the living room. I call home, the machine answers, and I say I'm staying over tonight, that I'll call back again later. Then I go into the kitchen, open the refrigerator, look for something to eat. There is a collection of things here, different efforts by her friends: a pan of spinach lasagna, fruit salad in a flowered bowl, banana bread wrapped in Saran Wrap and ribbon, wild strawberry Jell-O, half a baked ham. In the freezer is a container of homemade ice cream. Ruth's boss, Sarah, brought that. She said, "I was ready to put it in a container and all of a sudden I thought, wait—how big? If I put it in something small, will Ruth think I think she's going to die sooner?"

"I know," I said. "It's very confusing. This is all very confusing."

I break off a piece of the banana bread, sit at the little kitchen table to eat it, look out the window. There's a balcony off the kitchen with a turquoise Adirondack chair on it, many years old and sun-bleached to a pleasant pastel color. It faces the voluptuous rise of hills in the distance and looks to me to be alive and seeing. I hear a noise behind me; Ruth is coming slowly into the kitchen.

"Want some banana bread?" I ask.

She waves it away. "No. I hate banana bread. It's too suspicious-looking. I always thought the cooked banana looked like insect legs." I look at the piece of bread I've been eating. She's right. I put it down.

Ruth opens the refrigerator, scans the contents, closes the door without taking anything. "I don't recognize my own refrigerator anymore," she sighs. "All this sick-person stuff. Where are some lamb chops or something? Where's the fancy lettuce?" She is wearing her unlaced sneakers as slippers, a striped shirt over her nightgown. She hates slippers, lately, as she hates robes and bed jackets or bed trays and glasses left at her bedside. "If my brain goes and I can't do anything and they

16 bring those fucking bedpans into my house, shoot me,"
she told me.

She sits down at the table, subtly out of breath. "I
was sitting there the other day," she says, gesturing toward the balcony, "watching the sun set. And I was
thinking, I am so happy now. I love being alive. I just
want to *be* here. I want to stay. All that terrible anguish I
went through, it's gone! I'm happy now! Why can't my
body catch up to my head?" She looks at me. "Is it really too late, do you think?"

We have both heard the same information from
her doctor. We have both asked questions every which
way, trying to change the answers. They are always the
same. "Weeks to months, depending on what 'fails'
first." And yet.

"I don't know," I say. "I really don't. I mean, it's
a mystery how you got this, right? Nobody knows how
you got this. And nobody knows how those miracle
cures happen. They *do* happen!"

She nods, examines her hands. "I know they do."

"Have you been doing any of that imagery stuff?"

"Oh, yeah," she says. "I've been seeing myself as
strong and healthy. I see myself rowing, and running,
and dancing. And screwing, of course."

"You're supposed to see the bad cells getting attacked by good cells, too."

"Really?" She is sitting up straight, paying careful
attention.

"Well, I mean, remember that book we read, that
said you make your good cells killers of some kind?"

"Oh. Yeah, I remember. But that seemed so . . .
negative. Violent. I thought you were supposed to be

gentle. Positive and loving. You know, love yourself. Forgive yourself.''

"Well, that's true, too," I say. I listened with Ruth to a tape that someone had mailed her. We pulled her curtains, lay down on her bed, closed our eyes, turned it on. A woman spoke about envisioning yourself as a child, about holding yourself on your own lap and rocking yourself. We tried to be serious, but about halfway through we started laughing. I think it was the background music, all this silly tinkling, and then the insult of harps.

"Oh, I don't know what works!" I say now. "I mean, sometimes I sort of believe that stuff and sometimes I just don't.''

"Me, too," she sighs.

"Wait," I say, "I'll do it. I'll cure you. What we need here is something custom-made. You've never been a made-for-the-masses type." I stand up, hold my hands over her head, one above the other, make a low singing sound. It sounds sort of Native American. Maybe I've tapped into something I didn't know I knew. I squeeze my eyes shut, imagine walking in suddenly on Ruth's cancer. It is caught now, frozen like an animal in headlights. Now that it is seen, its plans spread out and revealed before it, I can tell it to stop, that's all. I remember meeting a man with cancer who told me that when he was diagnosed he came home, stood naked before his mirror and wept. Then he screamed, "Come out where I can see you! Let me *see* you!" And I do this now, see Ruth's outlaw cells, all of them, everywhere. They are asymmetrical, ragged-edged, leering. Their colors are dark red and purple, the colors of abuse.

18 They are slippery and quick and divide and divide and divide. But now I see them and I tell them to stop. That's all. Just stop. Why not? Why can't an ending to all this be subtle and arbitrary, when the beginning was that way? Her, sitting at a restaurant with me, with her bacon cheeseburger halfway up to her mouth, saying, "Oh, I've got another lump. Want to come with me to have it biopsied? Don't worry, they're never anything."

I open my eyes. Then I hug her. She is so thin now, like a suggestion of her former self. You have to be careful. I don't squeeze too hard, but I push a lot of feeling across the space between us. "There," I whisper. "Now you will start to heal."

She looks up at me and smiles and I see that she believes this might actually help. It is there as a slice of light in her eyes. She thinks this might actually help! And there's more: I believe it too, because it is all we have left. Oh, the stubbornness and the strength of hope. Every day that I am with her lately, I learn another staggering lesson. Everything about her is too much to bear: the delicacy of her wrist, the arrangement of her living-room furniture, the notices to renew magazine subscriptions that she gets in the mail. And yet we do bear it. She does, especially.

W e had gone to the late showing of *Sophie's Choice*. Ruth wanted to go when there weren't so many people. There were far fewer than at the seven-fifteen show, but she still insisted we sit in the back row. "I *hate* hearing people talking behind me," she said. "Don't you?"

I shrugged.

"I'm very particular about movies," she said. "You'll have to get used to it. You don't talk in movies, do you?"

"Just during the commercials."

"You don't mean the previews, do you?" She was nervous.

"No," I said. "I mean the commercials. Like when they tell you you can rent the place for parties. I don't talk during the previews. They're little movies."

"Exactly," she said, and settled in against her seat. Then she sat up again. "You don't chew gum or eat anything either, do you?"

"What do you take me for?" I asked.

"Forties talk," she said. "I love it." Then, as the lights came down, "Okay. Shhh." She reached into her purse, handed me two flowered handkerchiefs. "My grandmother's," she whispered. "You'll need them."

I held them up to my nose, to practice. They were softer than Kleenex, and smelled like lilacs and time. I couldn't wait to cry.

When the movie was over, before the lights had

20 finished coming up, an usher came and stood directly behind Ruth and me. "Please exit to your LEFT," he shouted. "And remember to deposit your GARBAGE in the clearly marked CANS on your WAY OUT!"

Ruth was right—the movie had left me feeling beat up; I was overwhelmed with sorrow. I was embarrassed for anyone to see me; two hankies hadn't been nearly enough. I saw that Ruth's eyes were swollen and red, and her face was splotchy with grief. But she was not embarrassed; she was furious. She walked quickly over to the usher, a sulky teenager who was leaning against the wall now, idly watching the stricken audience pass out of the theater and tonguing off one of his back teeth. "What is wrong with you?" she asked.

He blinked at her, stood up straight. His arms hung too long out of his uniform.

"Why do you have to scream about such inconsequential things?" she asked. "Why can't you just let us all have a moment of silence after a movie like this?"

The usher smiled nervously, started to answer.

"No," she said. "Have you seen this movie?"

He nodded yes.

"Well then, for Christ's sake!"

I touched her arm. "Maybe you have to be a mother to understand," I said.

She stared at me, wild-eyed. For a moment I thought she was going to start in on me, too. But all she said was, "Well, do you want to go get a drink?"

"Yes," I said, "but let's take a walk first." She went out ahead of me. I turned to the usher, who was making minute, spasmodic movements with his neck and shoulders, throwing off his embarrassment.

"Maybe you should wait just a minute to make your announcement," I said. "This movie is kind of . . . affecting."

"Well, I *guess,*" he said, and started down the aisle, patrolling for the garbage left beside the seats despite his post-film command. Of course this was to be expected. Give an order to someone in pain and they might easily rebel, just for the relief of something feeling good again.

———— ❧ ————

We walked to a nearby bar and sat at a table by the window. We ordered martinis. There was a polite moment of silence, each of us waiting for the other to initiate conversation. Then Ruth said, "Obviously, what I need is to get laid."

"Well," I said.

"That kid was just doing his stupid job. I know that. Jesus. He had bad acne, did you see? He's got enough to worry about."

"He should have given us a minute," I said. "Everybody was crying. I even saw a few men wiping their eyes."

"I know," she said, smiling, and then, "Are you good at dream interpretation?"

"I think it's always up to the dreamer what a dream means."

Ruth took a generous sip of her drink, leaned forward. "Last night I dreamed I came downstairs in the morning, and all my artwork was gone—every painting

22 was off the wall, the one I'm working on off the easel—hell, the *easel* was gone. Eric had locked everything in the basement, with a white sheet over it, like a shroud.''

I nodded. "He resents the time your art takes away from him.''

"He's killing me,'' she said.

T he back door opens, and Sarah is there, her expensive leather briefcase bulging. She hangs up her coat and kisses Ruth, then me. "I think it's going to snow. It's all of a sudden so cold.''

She sits down at the kitchen table with us, looks carefully at Ruth. "So. How are you?''

"I'm fine. Does it smell like snow?''

"Beats me,'' Sarah says. "How does snow smell?''

"I don't know . . . blue,'' Ruth says, and I know exactly what she means.

"How are you?'' Sarah asks again and Ruth says, "I *told* you I'm *fine*.''

No one says anything, and then Sarah says quietly, "I'm sorry.''

Ruth shrugs.

"It's just that I worry about you all day,'' Sarah says. "People ask about you, and I think . . .''

"You wonder if I'm dead yet, right?'' Ruth says.

"I don't know. Yes.''

"Well, don't worry about it,'' Ruth says. "I'll

call you right away when it happens. You'll be the first
to know."

There is a moment of silence, and then I say, "I think *I* should be the first to know."

"*I'm* her boss," Sarah says.

"But I'm her best friend."

"Maybe I won't die," Ruth says. "Ann gave me the cure today."

"How'd you do that?" Sarah asks.

"I stood over her and spoke in tongues and believed with all my heart and all my soul and all my mind that this won't happen." My voice shakes at the end of all this, and Sarah saves me. "Sounds too Catholic," she says. And then: "What's for dinner around here, anyway?"

"Nothing," Ruth and I answer together.

"Let's get lobster," Sarah says. "From that place right up the road from you. That's actually a very good restaurant."

Ruth shakes her head. "I don't want to go out."

"Then we'll get it to go."

Ruth frowns. "I don't think you can get lobster to go."

Sarah is at the phone already, dialing. "Why not?"

"I don't know. How do you get lobster to go?"

"You just tell them that's how you want it."

"They'll say no," Ruth says.

"Hold on a minute," Sarah says into the phone. Then, to Ruth, "No, they won't. I'll explain that this is an exceptional situation." Then, into the phone, she says, "I wonder if you could help me with a kind of unusual request."

24   Ruth smiles. "I always dreamed of being exceptional," she says. "Only not like this." She turns to
me. "I want some french fries from McDonald's, too."

"Okay," I say. "I'll go get them."

I put on my boots and my coat, and Ruth watches
me. She is, I know, remembering this: the intentional
pull of the coat over the shoulder, the confidence in saying you'll go somewhere and then just going. Nothing is
easy for her anymore. Everything has taken on an un-
welcome weight.

Sarah is off the phone; the lobsters will be ready to
be picked up in twenty minutes. "I'll go get the fries,"
I tell her.

"Get lots of catsup," Sarah says.

"Make sure they were *just* done," Ruth adds.

"Jesus," I say. "Anything else?"

"Get lots of those little salts," Ruth says.
"They're good."

I climb down the steps, thinking how good it will
taste, lobster and french fries, thinking about how I
would never ordinarily get take-out lobster. I am a re-
luctant beneficiary. I am the one standing at the base of
the high thing, shielding my eyes from the sun, shivering
with the challenge of the task I am watching someone
else do.

I pull into the McDonald's lot, tell the eager clerk
inside that I want three large orders of french fries.
"Now, they need to be perfect," I say.

She smiles, hesitates.

"I mean, were they just done?"

She looks over at the fryer. "They're about ten
minutes old, I guess. Ten, fifteen."

"I'll wait for a new batch," I say. "Just call me   25
when they're out."

"Okay," she says, and looks around me for the
relief of the next customer.

I sit at a booth, unbutton my coat, pick up a newspaper that someone has left behind. Today is Thursday.
Tomorrow is Friday. It scares me, the way tomorrow
keeps coming. I look in the paper for a good comic strip
to bring Ruth. All of them today would only hurt her
feelings. Try this sometime: read the comics as though
time were awfully short. You will be hard-pressed to
find anything funny. You will understand irony. You
will put down the paper and look at way the sun happens to be lighting the sky, and you will be thinking one
word: please.

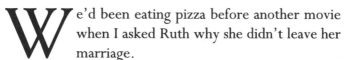

We'd been eating pizza before another movie
when I asked Ruth why she didn't leave her
marriage.

She shrugged. "You know. Michael. You met
him. You saw the size of his rib cage."

I had. I'd listened to his twelve-year-old lungs, a
courtesy medical call for Ruth, who was worried that
Michael's cold had progressed to pneumonia. He'd
taken off his wrinkled blue pajama top, smiled sweetly,
inhaled to the best of his ability. His lung sounds were
perfectly clear. He was fine—it was only a cold. I told
Ruth—who'd been leaning against the doorjamb with
clenched fists—that he was fine. She nodded, and her

26 face became free of the force that pulls down on mothers' eyes and mouths when their children are ill. "Thank you," she said, embarrassed by the tears in her eyes. But it was those tears that let me know we'd be friends, really.

"I know a guy who's a sociologist," I told her that night, "who says that kids by and large fare fine after divorce."

Ruth smiled. "Right. Where? Where is that?"

"He swears it's true. And he says a good divorce is better than a bad marriage."

"For who?" Ruth asked.

"I guess for everyone."

"Bullshit." She put down her fork, sighed. "Over and over, I've tried to say I want out. I've felt the words in my throat as if they're going to boil over. But I can't say them. I can't. I just stay. I stay and stay, and all of a sudden it's fifteen years later."

"I know," I said, and realized suddenly that I really did know. I too had had my moments of sitting on the side of the bed in the morning, looking at my husband getting dressed and wanting to take his arm and say, "Let's just stop this." One doesn't. One makes coffee.

"I came close, once," Ruth said. "We were out to dinner, Eric and I. We'd left Michael with a sitter, so we could be alone. But I don't know why—Eric might as well have been by himself. We were silent all the way there. Then, after we ordered, I kept trying to make conversation, but he wouldn't respond. I mean, he didn't even nod, he just sort of looked at me, picked at his teeth with a toothpick. And I thought, this is nuts.

I'm sitting here feeling desperate, and he won't say one fucking word. I felt this kind of . . . I don't know, panic, I guess. I saw that things were never going to change. And I just got up and walked out, left him there."

"Really?" I asked, a little thrilled.

She nodded. "And, you know, it felt so fine. That moment of simple truth. Seeing the situation as intolerable and for once really doing something about it."

"So what happened?"

"I just . . . started walking home. And I remember I felt so much *lighter*. I saw every leaf on every tree. The sun was setting, and I stood still and watched it, and it was beautiful. I felt air coming into me and air going out of me, and it was such a relief, as if someone had taken off a belt I'd forgotten about that was cinched way too tight. I was making a million plans, you know, how I'd sit on Michael's bed with him and tell him I was leaving his father, answer all his questions as honestly as I could—God! It felt so good to think about being completely honest! I thought about how I'd open my own checking account, how I'd give Eric all the electronics, everything, all I wanted was out. I walked for a few miles—I got blisters on my feet, but I didn't care—and then I saw a car pulling up, and it was Eric and I just . . . I got in."

"And?"

She sighed, looked away, then back at me. "He said he thought I'd gone to the bathroom, and the appetizers came and I didn't come back so he paid the bill and then drove around looking for me. He told me how embarrassed he was to be left like that. He asked if I were crazy."

"Well, did you tell him why you left?"

"Yeah, I told him why. And he told me it was an extreme and selfish reaction. That I was a hopeless romantic if I expected candles and hand-holding after all these years of being married. That if I wanted him to talk I should have said something."

"Jesus."

"And so," she smiled, held both hands up, surrender-style, "I apologized."

"But why?"

"Oh, God, I don't know. You don't know Eric. I can't describe how he does what he does. He's a lawyer, you know, he's good at manipulation. I mean, he'll actually say our relationship is fine, what the hell do I expect, and I'll end up agreeing. But I have made some progress. A few months ago I moved into my own bedroom. I said it was because Eric snored too loudly, but we both knew what it was. We eat together; we coparent; we share the bills. We're slightly hostile roommates."

"But that's horrible!" I said.

She shrugged. "Well, I look at Michael, and he's fine—he's doing well in school; he has friends; he sings in the shower. Just because I made a bad choice doesn't mean he has to suffer, too. He loves his father. And Eric says we're the same as most marriages except that we're more honest with each other. Look around, can you disagree?"

I swallowed, said nothing. If I wanted to argue against her position, what could I say? At the table next to us was an obviously married couple out to dinner. They stared vacantly past each other, engaged in conversation only when they needed to pass things to each other. All their lights were out. And what could I say about myself? That just last night, while my husband lay on top of me, I'd had tears of a terrible and too-familiar loneliness come to my eyes? That my husband—as usual—hadn't even known? That afterward he'd gone downstairs to read the newspaper while I lay in bed holding my pillow with a resigned loneliness like a child put to bed too soon? I was going through my own bad time lately.

But this is normal, isn't it? *C'est le mariage,* all that stuff. I mean, I have had this experience a thousand times: I am talking to a woman who is complaining bitterly about her husband. She is close to tears; her hands flutter, mothlike, around her face, ready to wipe away the evidence of her grief. Then I meet her husband, and he acts perfectly fine and friendly; and so does she. He puts his arm around her waist. She looks up at him, asks him about the plans they've made for the weekend. *Wait,* I always want to say. *Where is it, what you were talking about before?* The truth is, we usually only show our unhappiness to another woman. I suppose this is one of our problems. And yet it is also one of our strengths.

I told Ruth, "Listen, I know marriage has its ups and downs. But yours can't always be as terrible as you describe."

"Yes, it can," she said.

"But then you must be constantly . . . I mean, this has to take a terrific *toll* on you!"

"For a while," Ruth said, "I thought we could be saved. I would try therapy tricks, you know—active listening. Fair fighting, for God's sake. Really trying to see

30   things from his point of view. I would try to share things with him, tell him about what I was excited about, interested in. But it was the restaurant scene all over again. He would listen politely and walk away without saying a word and I would feel humiliation like a shower, you know? I would ask him to go places with me, and every time, he would refuse. And then I would ask him again! Nothing worked. There's no tenderness in me for him. And none in him for me.'' She smiled, looked up at me. ''He hates me.''

''He can't *hate* you,'' I said.

''Why not?''

I remembered the first time I met her husband. He was in the kitchen, leaning against the counter. He was blond, magazine-handsome, admirably muscular from the weightlifting he did every lunch hour. He wore a pair of khaki pants and a navy-blue sweater, loafers with no socks. The friendly look. But his brown eyes were a shut door. He kept his arms crossed tightly over his chest. Ruth told him my name, and when he said, ''Nice to meet you,'' I heard a thousand other things. I felt as though I'd come too early, or dressed wrong, or said an unforgivable thing.

''He did make me feel as if I was in trouble for something when I met him,'' I tell her now.

''Yes,'' she said. ''That's what I mean. That's how he is. You feel you've done something terribly offensive that only he can see. He won't tell you what it is. Because then he might have to forgive you.'' She sighed deeply.

''But there must have been something, once,'' I persisted. ''There was a reason you married him.''

"Of course," Ruth said. "I was pregnant."

"Oh, God."

"I know," she said. "But, listen. I don't care anymore. We have our little arrangement. I love my bedroom. It's gorgeous. French blues, a white wicker chair to read in by the window. I always have a box of Godiva chocolates under the bed. And it's such a relief not to have him all over me at night. He was a terrible lover, always. I don't know how he found the right place to get me pregnant."

We laughed, and then I said, "But . . . don't you miss sex?"

"I get plenty of that." She pulled a slice of pizza onto her plate, looked over at me. "Come on, you can figure it out."

I watched her take a bite of the pizza, then delicately wipe the corner of her mouth, and an image came to me. I saw Ruth and a man in bed together, naked. Ruth lay beneath him, her eyes closed, her hands knotted into fists of pleasure. A wide swatch of warm afternoon sun lay across the two of them and the rumpled sheets. Their sounds were quiet, earnest, intensely exclusionary. Orange peels lay in beautiful, two-tone disarray at the side of the bed. There was a romantic blurriness to the scene; and a wrenching kind of sweetness, too. My appetite disappeared.

"Does your son know?" I asked.

"About the others? No." She shook her head. "No, I'm incredibly discreet." She looked at her watch. "You know, I'm not that anxious to go to a movie. Let's go look at stuff that's too expensive for us to buy."

"Okay," I said. "We should try on evening gowns."

"Of course," she said.

"Who do you sleep with?" I asked.

She leaned back in her chair, smiled. "Why, Ann. I hardly know you."

———⟲———

I spill the french fries into a bowl when I get back to Ruth's, and we begin to eat them, slowly at first, then rapidly, even though Sarah has not yet returned with the lobsters. "These were better when they fried them in beef fat," Ruth says. "Everything's getting too goddamn good for you."

"I know."

"And even the things that are made the same taste different to me now. Do you think things taste different as you get older?"

"Of course," I say. "Potato sticks, Snoballs, they're nothing like they used to be."

"Peanut butter and jelly," Ruth sighs.

"But now we can appreciate martinis," I say.

"And semen."

I stop a french fry midair. "You don't *like* semen!"

She nods. "Yes, I do."

"Oh, God!"

"Don't you?"

"No!"

"Why not?"

"Well, it's . . . you know, like raw egg but even worse. It's too salty. And it's that terrible luke*warm!*"

"Well, what can I tell you? I always liked it." She takes another handful of fries. There aren't many left.

"Do you think we should cover these, save some for Sarah?" I ask, looking into the bowl.

"Nope. I don't wait anymore. They're here, right? We're here, right? Seize the moment."

I nod, think about all she is saying—and not. But what is "not waiting, anymore," really? What kind of hyperawareness does she live with? When she looks in the mirror, what does she see? What stands, see-through, behind her? When she puts down a fork, when she steps into her shoes, when she opens an envelope addressed to her—what is happening? Surely she must feel as though she is in another dimension. And surely she must be wiser, and capable of teaching us all something essential. It's as though she's wearing a robe that's hiding her real outfit.

"What's this all like, really?" I ask her now.

She stops chewing, looks at me. "What do you mean?"

"I don't know. I mean, I think about what it must be like to wake up at night, knowing all you know. And how everything . . . I don't know. I guess I wish you'd tell me more . . . inside stuff."

She stands up, pushes her chair in. "What do you want, Ann? A closer seat?"

"I didn't . . . I'm not asking—"

"Just be my friend, okay?" She starts toward her bedroom. "Just call me when the fucking lobster gets here." She turns around, her face flushed. "What's it

34 like for *you*, Ann? What's it like? What do *you* think about when you wake up? You're going to lose me, and I'm really important to you. The truth is I'm your only goddamn friend and I'm leaving. One-way ticket, Ann. And you have to stay here. Sometimes it's you I feel sorry for, not me." She is running out of breath. She looks around the room, then suddenly holds her hands out to me, palms up, as though she is giving me the whole world in the form of light and space. Then her arms collapse at her side, her head hangs down. "I think I don't know what the fuck I'm saying," she says. She begins to laugh, then to cry, jagged spasms of sound. "Jesus." She covers her face with her hands.

I cross the room and hold her, crying myself. "I'm sorry," I say. "I'm so sorry. Oh, I wish I could take a day for you. I wish we could trade for just one day."

She steps back from me, smiles bitterly. "No, you don't."

"Yes, I do. I do!"

"It might be the day I check out."

"I'd take the chance."

"The hell you would."

Nothing. Nothing except for the gigantic fact that she is right.

"We'll just eat, okay?" I say. "We'll just . . . eat."

"Okay. Okay." She embraces me again, her fingers press into my back, and I relish this small demonstration of strength. "I know what we should do," she says, pulling away from me and wiping the tears from her face. "Let's call L.D."

"Good idea," I say. Most times, L.D. is too much. But now she will be perfect.

"And bring those fries in here," Ruth says, heading again toward her bedroom. "Let's finish them. We'll call the restaurant and tell Sarah to go get more. Of course, whatever she brings, if L.D. is here, it won't be enough. We'll need to go get more again. It'll be like that Disney movie, where the buckets keep throwing water. What is that movie?"

"*Fantasia.*"

"Right," she says, crawling into her bed. "*Fantasia.* Do you know what I mean?"

I pull her quilt up over her, put the bowl of french fries in her lap, push my sneakers off my feet, climb up on the bed beside her. "Yeah, I know what you mean. Mickey couldn't keep up with the water, and we won't be able to keep up with the demand for french fries. It will just keep going on and on. Like frustration dreams—you know, you fall, you can't get up, and the truck keeps coming and coming."

"Yeah." She closes her eyes, then opens them. "Hey, Ann?"

"What?"

"*That's* what this is like."

"I know."

"You don't know."

"Okay."

"Call L.D."

"After Sarah."

Sarah wants to know why we need more fries.

36   "Because Ruth and I ate the ones I got," I said. "And because we're calling L.D. to come over."

    "Jesus," Sarah says. "Then we need about ninety more lobsters."

———— ❧ ————

R uth has friends like other people have wardrobes. I mean that there's someone for every occasion. Sarah is fine-boned, delicately beautiful, the kind of woman who can wear a perfectly tailored silk dress to take out the garbage and not spill a single thing on it. You know she's wearing makeup, but you can't find it. Her voice is low and smooth, conciliatory. She is management material through and through, clear-eyed and decisive. It was Sarah who organized all of us, made sure that there was a neatly typed roster of our names and phone numbers so we could reach one another, so we could make sure someone was always with Ruth.

    L.D. is a football-player-sized woman I've never seen in anything but checked flannel shirts and bib overalls—even on hot summer days. Her only variation is in the caps she wears—John Deere for dress up, sports teams for everyday. She is fearless, plain and simple. Ruth once said about L.D. that she appears to walk through life with her mouth wide open, taking in everything in her path. "I mean, she's a real life-*eater,*" Ruth said. And then, when I snorted, "I *guess!*" she hit me, saying, "She's the best. You should get to know her. She has incredible wisdom. She watches things, and she notices things you'd pass right over." Then, when I looked hurt, she added, "I mean, that anyone would pass over."

Ruth has friends she goes to bars to hear country-and-western music with, friends who invite her to chic little cocktail parties and openings, old college roommates who visit her for the weekend and play Scrabble. She rows on rivers, skis down mountains, sails on oceans, bikes down dirt roads for miles. Well, she used to. And anything she did, she had matching friends to do it with. Once, after she started chemotherapy, she called to tell me about a bike ride she'd taken. "We had to stop," she said. "My hair was flying off my head and causing visibility problems."

"*Was* it?" I asked.

"What," she said, laughing, "causing visibility problems?"

"No. Was it falling off?"

"Yeah," she said. "That's what happens. Remember when they told us that would happen?"

I remembered. But I thought she'd be standing over her bathroom sink, weeping. I should have known better. I should have known she'd be out on a bicycle, laughing.

"Are you really okay?" I'd asked.

"What do you mean? I mean, it doesn't *hurt*."

I was silent.

"It'll grow *back*," she said. "This wasn't unexpected. Right?"

I put my hand to my own hair, shaped a ponytail. "Yes," I said. "Right."

I have a bunch of rocks on my kitchen windowsill

38   that I collected for their beauty, for their silent perseverance. After I finished talking to Ruth, I went to look at them. Then I picked one up and squeezed it.

L.D. is knocking at the door. You can tell because the apartment is reverberating with the sound of it. She lets herself into the hallway, comes into the bedroom, nods to me, and then to Ruth. "Get the fuck out of bed," she says.

"Can't. I'm really tired, L.D."

L.D. nods, pulls out a small package from her pocket. "For you," she says. Ruth opens it and finds pearl earrings, studs.

"Put them on," L.D. says, settling herself down on the floor beside Ruth's bed.

"Oh, they're beautiful," Ruth says. "Thank you, L.D."

"I thought they were, you know . . . you," L.D. says, then turns to me fiercely. "Don't you think so?"

"Absolutely," I say. "Uh-huh."

And they are. They glow prettily against Ruth's earlobes. They are just the right size. I wonder what L.D. said when she bought them. Probably nothing. Probably she just pointed, and the clerk wrapped them up fast.

"We ordered out some dinner," Ruth tells L.D. "Can you stay?"

"What'd you get?"

"Lobster and french fries. Want some?"

"It's a start," L.D. says. Then, stretching, she asks Ruth, "Have you been outside today?"

Ruth shakes her head no.

"Put your coat on," L.D. says.

"I'm not kidding, L.D., I'm tired," Ruth says. "I don't think I can do the steps."

"I'll do them for you," L.D. says. She stands up, swoops Ruth up off the bed, carries her to her closet. Ruth, laughing, pulls her coat off the hanger and wraps it around herself, and L.D. starts downstairs. "Don't come," L.D. says over her shoulder to me.

"I'm *not*," I say, though I suddenly ache to.

"We need to talk," L.D. says. "Nothing against you."

"I understand," I say, and I do. It's hard to be private with Ruth anymore; anyone can and does show up at any time. But L.D., in her usual way, mows over obstacles. She wants to be alone with Ruth. And so she will be.

I watch from the bedroom window as L.D. carefully sets Ruth on her feet outside. There is a thin layer of snow on the ground already and L.D. is making a tiny snowman. I can only see Ruth's back, but I believe she is smiling. Then L.D. is standing close to her, embracing her, and saying things in her ear. Ruth pats L.D.'s back and her hand looks even smaller than usual. Then L.D. turns her toward the door, smacks her butt, and they are on their way back upstairs.

The bit of fresh air has colored Ruth's face, and her eyes look the way they used to—ready for action, in on the joke. She was right to call L.D.

Just as we settle Ruth back in her bed, we hear

40   Sarah coming up the stairs. She calls out hello, goes into the kitchen. There is the sound of paper bags rustling, then soft swearing. All of Ruth's friends are terrible— or wonderful, depending on how you look at it— swearers. I go into the kitchen, and find Sarah standing back from the kitchen table, hands on her hips. "Look at all those disgusting antennae sticking out," she says. "I hate them. I should have had them beheaded."

"L.D.'s here," I say.

"Oh, okay," she says. We call L.D. and she comes into the kitchen, takes a beer from the refrigerator, drinks it down, and then cheerfully begins to twist the heads off the lobsters. Sarah and I don't watch. We set places on Ruth's bedroom floor: lay a tablecloth down, put a vase of flowers in the center of it. Ruth won't eat without them. Also, the dishes must not match. "Stupidest idea I ever heard of," Ruth once told me. "Don't you want to see something different when you look around the table? All chicken breasts, all on the same yellow plates. Ridiculous!"

We use pottery dishes: plates, bowls, cups. The colors are pale blues, earthy browns, off-whites. There are leaf imprints, fragile paintings of weeds leaning into the wind, abstract smears of paint that seem to change meanings depending on your mood. Naturally, no two things are alike.

L.D. appears, holding a tray full of decapitated lobsters. She sets them down, picks one up and cracks its back. "Where's the broccoli?" she asks, looking over our spread. "She's supposed to eat broccoli and carrots all the time. How the fuck can she get better eating french fries?"

Sarah and I steal a look at each other. It is a careful thing, full of guilt. Only yesterday Sarah told Ruth she should start thinking about where she wants to be buried. I have suggested she might want to write something to be read at her funeral. Because no matter how often I've let hope rise up in me, I don't really believe Ruth can make it. But L.D. rejects the notion of Ruth not overcoming all of this. She brings her Chinese herbs, books about miracles, crystals to wear around her neck, exotic broths. She insists that Ruth be outside for a time every day, to suck in great mouthfuls of air, to feel her feet on the earth, thus staking her claim to it. Who knows what the right way is? Every time I see L.D., I think of a story I read to Meggie when she was younger. It was based on a Chinese myth about how a hole in the sky got mended. I always got an image, reading that story, of a circle of black-haired women wearing beautiful red silk kimonos touched here and there with gold. They were sewing and smiling; humming soft, high songs to themselves. They held shiny silver needles, long and curved slightly upward, and they wove them delicately in and out of the air. What did they use for thread? Only their belief. And guess what? The sky held. Is holding still. Just look.

It was Indian summer, late October. Ruth called and suggested we have a picnic. It was Saturday; both our husbands were home; none of us had plans. "Should we let everybody come?" I asked.

"No."

I smiled. "Maybe we'd have fun."

"Come on, I just want to go and find a beautiful place and relax."

"Okay," I said. "I'll come get you. What should I bring?"

"Let's see," she said. "Wine, cheese, bread, fruit, those cream-cheese brownies from the bakery. A blanket."

"Oh, fine. And what are you bringing?"

"Really good gossip."

"Oh," I said. "Okay. As long as it's fair."

I told my husband I was going out with Ruth and he said, "Good. Because I don't want to do anything today. Stay gone a long time. Go to a fabric store—I'll see you at dinner."

He was both kidding and not, assuming a man's usual position of benign inscrutability. We had minor tiffs almost every weekend, because I wanted to go places and he wanted to relax. It was a common enough domestic problem, but it was beginning to feel like more than that to me. I'd told Ruth that sometimes I thought Joe hated me, too, that in fact on my darker days I thought all husbands hated all wives, that it was a natural part of any marriage that lasted more than two weeks.

"It's not just husbands and wives," she'd said. "Men just *can't* like women. Even if they wanted to like us—which they don't—they're too jealous. They want to be like us, and they can't be. And they know they need us more than we need them, and it drives them crazy. Much of this, of course, is subconscious." Then, looking at me, "It's *true!*"

"Oh, let's just get an apartment together and be roommates," I'd said.

"Do you want to?" she asked quickly.

I laughed, embarrassed. "No, I . . . was joking."

"Ah," she'd said. "I see."

Eric answered the door when I came to get Ruth. He invited me into the living room, then called up the stairs that I was there. "Going out for a picnic, huh?" he asked.

I nodded. He was a powerful man, in the bad sense of the word. He made my hands feel huge, made my voice disappear.

"I guess I just don't much like picnics," he said.

I felt a momentary twinge of annoyance—had she asked him first?

Ruth came downstairs, smiled at me, then turned to Eric. "We'll be back," she said. Her voice chilled me. There was nothing dramatic you could point to—it wasn't cruel, or sarcastic, or on the edge of anything. But there was a tension you could feel—not only in her voice, but in the space between the two of them. It was nearly unbearable.

44   When we got into my car, I said, "Jesus, it's *thick* between the two of you."

"What is?"

"The *tension,* my *God,* Ruth."

She lowered the visor to look in the little mirror there. "Something's in my eye," she said. "It hurts like hell."

"You want me to wait?"

"No," she said, looking back at the house. "Go."

We found a place by the river. The leaves were heartbreaking—too beautiful. I collected a pile while Ruth laid out the blanket and our food. Then I brought them back, stacked them neatly beside me and put a rock on top of them.

"What are you going to do with those?" Ruth asked.

I shrugged. "I don't know. I do this every year, collect some. I just want them."

"It's outrageous, isn't it?" Ruth asked.

"What?"

"Fall. It's outrageous! I really belong in California, but I stay in Wisconsin for the leaves. I mean, don't you just want to stand in the middle of all this and scream, 'Wait a minute! Wait a minute!' "

I lay down on the blanket, sighed. "Yes. Exactly. I take walks with Meggie and I keep saying 'Look at that! Look at *that!*' And she rolls her eyes and says, 'I *know,* Mom.' She's so young, and she's already a cynic. But I can't help it. I want to make sure she sees! All I do is embarrass her. She and Joe both think I'm too emotional. They think I'm sort of crazy.''

"Show me,'' Ruth said. "I don't think you're crazy.''

I handed her the pile of leaves and watched as she looked at them. She held them up to the light, turning them this way and that, nodding. "This is a wonderful collection,'' she said. "You got the best ones here.''

"Thank you,'' I said, and something inside of me . stopped looking down.

"You're welcome.'' She picked up the bottle of wine, pulled the cork. "Want some?''

I held my cup out. And as I drank, I thought about the kind of internal relaxation, the wide relief you feel when someone says, "I know,'' and you believe them. I'd never had a friend like Ruth. I was shy; I had trouble trusting people; and I'd always spent most all of my time alone. I liked the immediate and easy intimacy that Ruth and I shared, the way we seemed to see so many things alike. I thought about how good it was to know I'd finally found a friend I would have for the rest of my life. We'd already decided that when our husbands kicked, we'd open a nursing home for hip women. "No rocking chairs,'' Ruth had said. "No fucking bingo.''

When we were through eating, we lay head to head under the canopy of trees to watch the drifting leaves, the acrobatic squirrels, to listen to the rushing sounds of the river. We were quiet for a long time, half asleep, and then Ruth said, "I met my first lover in the art class I teach."

I said nothing at first, then asked, tentatively, "He was your student?"

"Yes. He had intense blue eyes, and he sat in the back so he could act up. That alone made him nearly irresistible. He also painted differently from anything I'd ever seen. He said he'd had no experience, but I don't know . . . Anyway, there was this terrific attraction that neither of us did anything about until the last day of class."

"How tasteful of you."

"Well, I don't know if anything would have happened then, either," she said. "It was just that we were standing in the parking lot after class, and I just all of a sudden . . . I said, 'Oh, God, I'm just *crazy* about you,' and threw my arms around him and kissed him for about an hour and a half. My purse got stuck between us, and we were both trying to act like it wasn't there. He was kind of upset at first, he knew I was married and everything, but then he said something like, 'Oh, I've thought about this so many times, do you know how much I've wanted to . . .' and he flung my purse to the ground and grabbed my ass and kissed me again and it was all so tempestuous and *won*derful.''

I felt a stirring in my stomach. "So did you . . . go back to his place?"

She sighed. "No. We didn't know what to do. It was weird. We exchanged phone numbers, and then we waited a while. I think he called me a few times, I called him, and then we met for lunch and *then* we went back to his place. I stayed until I had to go home for Michael."

"Wasn't it hard?" I asked. "I mean, to shift gears like that?"

"Yeah, it was really hard. I felt terrible, giving Michael a snack on his little dinosaur plate, looking at his schoolwork. His teacher had given him a sticker on one of his papers and I thought, What would *she* think? And the worst part was that night Eric wanted to make love."

"Did you?"

"More or less. I mean, I'm sure nothing seemed different to him. For it me, it was awful. But after the first lie, it gets so much easier. It's disappointing, in a way, how easy it is."

"Are you still seeing him?" I asked.

Ruth sat up, shook her hair back over her shoulders. "Nah. He was three guys ago." She looked at me. "Is this terrible? It's terrible, isn't it?"

"I don't know."

"I think it's just that at some point I made a conscious decision that I was not going to be without pas-

48 sion in my life. I need it like water. And I'm not really promiscuous, honest.''

I smiled.

''I'm not!''

''I believe you!''

She looked my face up and down. ''Did you ever think about having an affair?''

''I guess everybody does,'' I said.

''No, not everybody does.''

''Well, I have.''

''Why haven't you done it?''

''Well, God, think of it. Think of all that could happen if you got caught.''

''If the only reason you're not doing it is because you think you'll get caught, you might as well do it,'' Ruth said. She bit into an apple, stopped chewing to say, ''Really.''

''That's not the only reason I don't do it,'' I said.

''Uh-huh,'' she said. ''What are the other reasons?''

I said nothing.

''You won't get caught,'' she said. ''I can promise you that. I've been doing this for six years, Ann. It doesn't take much intelligence to not get caught. Although, at first, you really wish you would.'' She looked down to trace a design in the dirt. ''You have this idea that maybe it could help.'' She looked up, smiled bitterly, then smoothed her hand over her drawing to erase it.

W e are finished eating. Laid out on Ruth's floor are the remains of our meal. There are broccoli stalks, courtesy of L.D., who went out and got that as well as the makings for hollandaise sauce. There are ravaged orange-red lobster shells lying in a steep pile, and gigantic bowls with sticky pools of leftover ice cream at the bottom. L.D. ate an amount that could most kindly be called inspirational and now, satisfied, leans against the wall picking her teeth with a matchbook cover. Sarah, long legs silkily crossed, is sitting in a chair by Ruth's bed, idly flipping through a magazine. I am stretched out on the bed beside Ruth, my jeans unbuttoned and unzipped, even my bra unhooked. "I'm sick," I groan.

L.D. snorts. "What a wimp."

"I'm not a wimp!"

"Yes, you are," Ruth says.

Sarah puts down the magazine, looks at her watch, stands up and stretches. "I've got to go," she sighs. She leans over to kiss Ruth. "I'll see you tomorrow." She nods to L.D.; then, as she is pulling on her coat, asks, "What does L.D. stand for, anyway? I never heard you say."

L.D. pushes herself up off the floor, heads for the bathroom. "You never will, either." She slams the door shut.

Ruth smiles. "Loosely translated: Good-bye, Sarah. Great seeing you."

50   "Do you know what it stands for?" Sarah asks quietly. At the same time Ruth shakes her head, we hear L.D.'s muffled voice. "No, she doesn't. Nobody does."

"Oh. Well. Good night then, Lucinda Diane," Sarah calls.

Nothing.

"Laura Dee Dee?"

The toilet flushes, the door bangs open, and L.D. reappears. "Fuck you, Sarah."

"Oh, no, that can't be it," Sarah says. "That would be F.Y." She smiles, embraces all of us, and is gone.

"Does that woman even have to use deodorant?" L.D. asks.

"Oh, come on, she's great," Ruth says. "You should see her apartment. It's so . . . comfortable. She's really learned how to enjoy living alone. I wish I'd learned how to do that."

"You're learning now," L.D. says. "Look at this: every night, a fucking party."

"Well," Ruth sighs, "not a *fuck*ing party. Unfortunately." She takes her Red Sox hat off the bedpost and puts it on her head. Then she gets out of bed to start gathering up the dirty dishes.

"We'll do that," L.D. says. "You . . . meditate."

I wash the dishes, L.D. dries. We don't have to guess anymore where things go; the place is beginning to feel like ours, too. The kitchen radio is turned on low to a country-and-western station. The stupidity of the lyrics is comforting.

When we are done, L.D. hangs the dishtowel

evenly over the rack. "Are you staying with her to-   51
night?"

"Yeah."

"Call me if . . . you need to."

"I will."

We go back to the bedroom and L.D. sits down
beside Ruth. "Tonight, before you go to sleep," she
says, "I want you to think of all the things you want to
do tomorrow."

"L.D."

"What?"

"What *does* L.D. stand for?"

I stand back respectfully, but stay in the room. I
want to hear.

"Someday," L.D. says, "I'll get drunk and tell
you."

"Oh, you're such a tease."

"No, I'm not," L.D. says, and there is such
honesty and innocence to her voice I want to hold her.
The bedside lamplight is a rich golden color, and it is
falling on her face in a way that makes it seem gilded.
For a moment, L.D. looks to me like an angel. Another
case of illusion only being the larger truth.

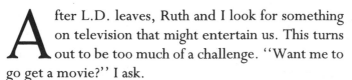

After L.D. leaves, Ruth and I look for something
on television that might entertain us. This turns
out to be too much of a challenge. "Want me to
go get a movie?" I ask.

"No." She sighs, looks around her room. "You

52 know, I never thought dying would be boring. Did you? I mean, I find myself getting to this place of readiness. It's a kind of deep peace, that I never felt before. And so I lie there thinking, okay, I guess this is it, this is a good time, go ahead; and then the phone rings and it's somebody wanting to steam clean my wall-to-wall carpeting, which of course I don't even have. And I want to say, 'Oh, stop with this carpet nonsense. Listen to me. You've got to be careful. Say all you need to say, right away. You have no idea how fragile this all is!' But of course all I say is 'No thank you.' " She smiles. "Who would have thought it would be like this?"

I am quiet for a moment, then say, "Know what I'm really glad about, though?"

"What?"

"That you get to be peaceful, sometimes."

"Oh, yeah, when I'm not terrified, I'm real peaceful. And you know what else? It's such a rich thing. It's so . . . good. And sometimes I think, God, my life has taken these awful turns, but they're also sort of wonderful. I mean, the constant presence of you all—my friends . . ." Her eyes fill and I put my hand on her arm. She is talking too much. She's too short of breath.

"Rest a minute," I say. "Stop talking."

"No," she says. "Let me." She turns to face me earnestly. "Sometimes I feel as if I want to stay sick so I can keep all this."

"Oh, God, don't say that!"

"I don't want to die, but sometimes I wonder . . . Wouldn't it be terribly anticlimactic if I went back to normal? I mean, for all of us?"

I am lying on Ruth's sofa in one of those states where your body seems asleep but your mind has other ideas. I turn on the little lamp on the table, look at my watch. Three forty-seven. I sit up, look around, wish that I were home. Then I could go into Meggie's room and watch her sleep, set myself right. I worried, when I was pregnant, that it would be so hard to be a mother, that it would drive me crazy to be needed so much. I never suspected that it would be I who needed Meggie more.

I pull a magazine from the pile in the handwoven basket Ruth keeps under her coffee table. The cover advertises a story about preventing breast cancer. I wonder if she has seen it. I put the magazine at the bottom of the pile, go out into the kitchen and turn on the light. I want some tea, but I don't want to wake Ruth up by running water.

Assuming she is alive.

I stand up, then sit back down. Then I stand up again, tiptoe into her bedroom. She is turned away from me, but I can hear her breathing. I see moonlight lying against the back of her bald head, pooled in the small valley at the top of her neck. They are so graceful and beautiful, necks, so full of a kind of combined strength and vulnerability. I wish we could get over our horror of baldness and appreciate instead the tender revelations it provides.

When Ruth first heard about how the chemo

54   would probably make her lose her hair, she asked me if I would go with her to get a wig when the time came. I said I would, but I also asked her if she were sure that's what she wanted to do.

"What else would I do?" she asked.

"I don't know," I said. "If it were me, I think I'd be more of a scarf type. Or just walk around bald. I mean, it's kind of a badge of honor, isn't it?"

"You didn't think I should get fake boobs, either," Ruth said.

"I know. Same reason. Except what you did is just as good." What Ruth did was to get prostheses three times the size she was—she went from a 34 A to a 38 C.

She waited until her hair was quite thin before she decided it was time for a wig. And even then, on the way to get it, she asked me, "*Do* you think I have to get one now? Does it look really bad?"

She was driving, and I looked over at her and the sun was coming through her hair, making it look like an aura. I thought it was beautiful. "It just looks as if you have real thin hair," I said.

"That's what I think, too," she said. "But I'd better get one now in case it gets worse."

I was carrying a magazine I thought would give us ideas for wig styles. Ruth had said she wanted something really short for a change.

"Look at this woman on the cover," I told her, holding up the magazine. "Her hair is pretty short, and she looks great."

Ruth snuck a glance, then looked back at the road.

"Yeah," she said. "That's what I'll do." Then she sighed and I was careful not to look at her. I turned on the radio, and we rode the rest of the way there without talking.

———— ❧ ————

The place was located in a suburban medical building. When we got into the lobby, we looked at the roster of names to see what office we were supposed to go to. A man in a uniform seated behind a small desk asked, "May I direct you ladies?" We didn't even look at him, even when he asked again. We were full enough of what we had to do.

The sign on the door said PATRICIA LOOMIS, which Ruth and I agreed was highly unimaginative. "It should say BALD BUSTERS or something," Ruth said. "Or HAIR TODAY, GONE TOMORROW."

She took in a breath, opened the door, and announced herself to the blank-faced receptionist wearing a show-off ponytail. Then we sat on an overstuffed sofa with a coffee table in front of it that held a book called *Cancer and Beauty*.

"Oh, man, look at this," Ruth said, picking the book up and flipping through it. Mostly it was tricks for tying scarves. *Don't be afraid to get creative!* the book said. She rolled her eyes and put it down. There was a basket of fake geraniums on the table, too, and Ruth fingered one of the thick green leaves in disgust. "In keeping with the fake-o theme, I suppose," she said. She crossed

56 her legs, swung her foot. "I'm a nervous fucking wreck," she said quietly, not looking at me.

"Me, too." I looked down into my lap, saw my fingers squeezing a knuckle.

Finally, a woman came out and called Ruth's name. As we followed her down the hall, she turned around and looked critically at Ruth. "Have you been walking around like that?" she asked.

I thought, oh, God, don't cry, Ruth, and she didn't. She said, "Well, of course I've been walking around like this. Jesus Christ. What else? If I had a wig, I wouldn't be here now, would I?"

Yeah, I thought. Yeah! And then I thought, what is someone like that doing working in a place like this, where women with broken hearts come?

After she'd brought us to the fitting room, the woman left to get some sample wigs. Ruth was seated in a swivel chair before a huge mirror, a setup like those they have in beauty salons. There was a hand mirror there, too, so she'd be able to inspect the back of her head.

"I think that woman is premenstrual," I said.

"I think she's prehistoric. Did you see the wrinkles in her neck?"

"Yeah," I said, though I hadn't.

When the woman returned, she handed Ruth a hairnet. Ruth pulled it on, then turned her head this way and that, looking at herself in the mirror. "I look great," she said. "Like a cafeteria worker."

"Give me some of that, uh, American chop suey," I said.

Ruth smiled. I smiled. The woman frowned and I wanted to drive something wide and sharp into her softest part. On the way out of the place, I asked her, "Why do you have to be such a bitch? Why do you have to make a hard thing harder?"

"I beg your pardon?" she asked coldly.

"You should," I said.

"Don't worry about it," Ruth said, paying for the wig she'd ordered—a short, dark-brown one—with her MasterCard. "Rush this order, okay?" she said. "Put it on the next rocket. I just found out I'm not supposed to be walking around like this."

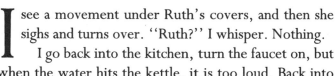

I see a movement under Ruth's covers, and then she sighs and turns over. "Ruth?" I whisper. Nothing.

I go back into the kitchen, turn the faucet on, but when the water hits the kettle, it is too loud. Back into the living room, I stand before the bookcase, looking for something to read. Ruth has different pieces of art mixed in with the books. There is pottery: a short, round vase the color of eggshell; a small box with a geranium leaf imprint; a deep-blue bowl holding dried rose petals, a purple shoe with unfurled wings at the heel. There are tiny oils of individual flowers. I find something that I made years ago, the one time I tried to use clay. I pick it up and hold it, close my eyes, think maybe all it requires is a certain kind of belief and you really can go back in time. I wish hard, and open my

58   eyes. Naturally, I am nowhere else. I am actually sort of surprised.

I always think incipient miracles surround us, waiting only to see if our faith is strong enough. If I am standing at a traffic light before I cross a street, I stare at the people on the other side, thinking, why can't we just concentrate, and change places? And I have a real belief that this kind of thing will eventually come to be, this convenient kind of transmigration. "Come over for dinner, why don't you?" we will say into the phone to our friends in California when we are in Wisconsin. And moments later they will appear, shiny with stardust, briefly shaken but mostly without memory of how it happened that they arrived. We won't have to understand it; it will just work, like a beating heart, like love. Really, no matter how frightened and discouraged I may become about the future, I look forward to it. In spite of everything I see all around me every day, in spite of all the times I cry when I read the newspaper, I have a shaky assurance that everything will turn out fine. I don't think I'm the only one. Why else would the phrase "Everything's all right" ease a deep and troubled place in so many of us? We just don't know, we never know so *much,* yet we have such faith. We hold our hands over our hurts and lean forward, full of yearning and forgiveness. It is how we keep on, this kind of hope.

I turn out the light, lie back down on the sofa, close my eyes, and try to remember everything about the time Ruth wanted to help me make some pottery. You take what you can get. That is another one of the lessons here.

W e went to the studio she taught in one snowy Sunday afternoon. She shared it with a potter, and she'd told me I could sculpt while she painted. She turned the radio up loud to a rock station and brought out some off-white clay, put it in a mound before me. "Go ahead," she said, patting it affectionately. Then she went to her easel, picked up her brush.

"Go ahead what?" I asked. "I don't know how to do anything."

"Make it up," she said. "That's what the first guys did."

I made a ball. "There."

She shrugged. "Okay."

"Well, *help* me," I said.

"What's in you?" she asked.

"What do you mean?"

"Jesus," she said. "You've got to loosen up."

I sat still, waiting for inspiration. I hoped I'd recognize it if it did come. I felt nothing. Finally, I said, "Okay, I'm going to make a pot to piss in. Then I can never say I don't have a pot to piss in."

"There you go!"

She worked on her painting, while I created, for reasons unknown, a dog on a raft.

At one point, she came to stand in front of me. "A dog? On a *raft*?"

I blushed.

"I love it!" she said.

I shrugged, smashed it down.

"What did you do that for?" she asked, incredulous.

"I don't know. It was stupid."

She sat down across from me, took the clay, examined it. Nothing was left. "Somebody did something to you around this creativity thing, right?"

"What do you mean?"

"Somebody got you all inhibited about doing anything creative."

"Oh, boy," I said. "Art therapy. How much is this going to cost me?"

"Can you remember anything that happened?" She was serious, staring intently at me.

"Actually," I said, "I do remember one thing. I think I was about five or six, and we were drawing in school, and I kept standing up to do it. I could work better that way. The teacher told me to sit down, but I kept forgetting—I was real excited. So she took my chair away, and then every time we had art after that, she took it again. I always had to stand, every time we had art. Of course it was highly amusing for everyone but me."

"See?" Ruth said. She handed me back the clay. "Take it all back. Get it back."

"I don't know what you mean," I said.

"Sure you do."

I made another dog on a raft. I showed Ruth and she put her hands on my shoulders and kissed me full on the mouth. There is a pure place in all of us that makes no judgments about anything, ever. That place recog-

nized what Ruth did as being absolutely right. The rest
of me was nervous. I stepped back, blushing, and she
laughed.

She had my piece glazed and fired and, when I said
I didn't want it, she kept it. She tied a tiny bandanna
around the dog's neck, laid a baby Frisbee at his feet.

Seeing that piece again now, I realize how much I
need Ruth. She hears my unspoken sentences. My stomach contracts, and I feel the terrible sense of claustro-
phobia that comes from knowing there is nothing you
can do about a situation that is intolerable but tolerate
it. I let myself cry a little, quietly; and then, mercifully,
I go to sleep.

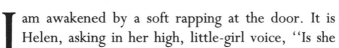

I am awakened by a soft rapping at the door. It is
Helen, asking in her high, little-girl voice, "Is she
up?"

"No," I whisper, stepping back to let her in. I
point to the kitchen and we go in there, shut the door to
keep things quiet.

"There's a good couple inches of snow out
there," Helen says. "It's so exciting!" She slides her
coat and boots off. She is wearing two different-colored
socks.

"Nice look," I say.

"Oh, I'm like this all the time, lately," Helen
says, looking down at her socks. "I forget what the hell
I'm supposed to be doing. I miss my exits on the free-
way. Sometimes I even answer the phone and then for-

62 get I'm on it." She puts a bag on the center of the table. "I brought six million muffins."

"I've gained five pounds from all this goddamn stress," I said. "I can't have any."

"Ten," Helen says, pointing to her stomach. "All I can wear are sweat outfits anymore. But I don't care. I'm making coffee and then I'm eating a lot."

Helen is Ruth's oldest friend. They met in junior high school, were on the cheerleading squad together. Helen's mother was part Cherokee, and the bones in Helen's face are the kind your eyes can't leave. She is one of the most unusually beautiful women I've ever seen, and also one of the least aware of her own loveliness. She works in a bookstore, sits on a stool behind the counter reading all day, and makes customers wait if she's at a good part.

When the coffee is done, we both take a chocolate-chip muffin. We are on our second when Ruth comes into the kitchen. "Hey," I say. "Want some coffee? And a muffin?"

"Sure," she says, and sits down. She actually looks good, well rested, pink-cheeked. She has her hat on, her lumberjack shirt, kneesocks under her nightgown. She has washed her face and brushed her teeth: I can smell Listerine. We sit at the little table in the pale-yellow, winter-morning sun; and we eat and talk and laugh, and nobody says anything about illness or death or dying. It is so close to the old way. I have the sensation of both sitting at the table and floating above it.

Helen is telling us about her new boyfriend. His name is Rudolph. He makes pizzas. But his real job is writing poetry. "He read me this weird one last night,"

Helen said. "I couldn't make sense out of it at all, and I
knew he really wanted me to understand it."

"So what'd you tell him?" Ruth asks.

"Oh, I just made myself get tears," Helen says. "I can do it easy. Look." She sits still for a moment, looks down, and when she looks up again, she does indeed have tears welling up magnificently in her eyes.

"Wow," Ruth says.

"Naturally," Helen says, "when I do that, I don't have to say anything. He just thinks I'm moved beyond words." She rolls her eyes, reaches for another muffin. "I don't know how long I can keep this guy around. It's kind of exhausting crying all the time."

There is a feeling of a beat being missed when she says this. We none of us acknowledge it. We want to keep going in the direction we were headed.

There is another knock at the door, and Sarah comes in. "I just have a minute," she says. She hands Ruth a slip of paper. "This is what I forgot to give you yesterday," she says. "All of these are places where you can get buried for what you can afford."

I have been on an airplane twice where it suddenly lost altitude. It felt just like this.

"Oh," Ruth says. "Okay. Good. Thanks." She puts her muffin down, looks at me. "Can you take me to see one of these before you go home?"

I nod, feel two parallel lines of an ache start in my throat. If there is one thing I hate lately, it's the present.

While Ruth goes to get dressed, Helen says, "I'll come with you guys if you want."

"I wish you hadn't done this right now," I tell Sarah. "We were finally not talking about death."

64

"Well, I'm sorry," she says. "It has to be done. She asked me to help her. It really does have to be done."

Neither Helen nor I say anything.

"I have to get to work," Sarah says. "Tell her I'll call her later."

After the door shuts, I say quietly, "No. I won't tell her anything. Just leave her alone."

"God," Helen says. "She's relentless."

"Oh, she's just . . . I mean, it does have to be done," I say. "She's the only one of all of us who's taken care of the details of all this necessary . . . crap."

"I know," Helen says. "But sometimes I hate her for it."

"Me, too."

Ruth comes into the kitchen, picks up the phone, and while Helen and I drink coffee, calls the first person on the list, tells them what she's looking for. "I don't want to be too crowded in," she says. There is a long pause, during which she nods and says, "Um-hum. Okay. Okay." Then she says, "Breast cancer." And then, "Well, I'm only forty-three. Which is really terrible."

—— ❧ ——

We were sitting in a restaurant, talking about Ruth's current boyfriend. She was excited, her eyes wide, her cheeks flushed with color. She was wearing a new sweater, new earrings, new underwear. She was going to have dinner with me, then go and spend the rest of the evening with him. She'd told Eric we were going to a late movie. "Don't forget, if it ever comes up, that we saw that movie together," she said.

"Okay."

"And don't tell Joe."

I said nothing.

"You don't tell him about this stuff, do you?"

I didn't answer.

"Jesus! What do you tell him for?"

"Well, what do you think, Ruth? You think he's going to tell Eric? He never sees Eric!"

"Things can slip, Ann. Shit!"

"Maybe I have a different relationship with my husband than you do with yours," I said.

She looked at me, said nothing.

"I mean, I do tell him things. We are able to speak to one another."

She picked up the check, dug in her purse for her wallet. "Fine."

"It's nothing against you, Ruth! Why do I have to lie, too?"

"You don't. You're right. I'm sorry."

"I don't believe you."

"I'm sorry! I am! I won't ask you to lie any more, okay?"

I put my money on the table. "Okay." I looked down for a long moment, then back up. "I'm jealous, okay? I'm jealous of you. I can't remember the last time I was excited to see a man. I'm sick of folding fucking laundry for entertainment. I feel three hundred years old. I never even wear perfume anymore."

66   "Well, get some," Ruth said.
"Get some what?"
She smiled. "There you go."

T
he graveyard we look at is small, surrounded by a low, black, iron fence that leans slightly inward.

"I hate it," Ruth says. "It looks like a vampire lot. There might as well be fog swirling around our feet, wolves baying in the distance." She turns to Helen and me. "Don't you think? I don't want Michael to have to come here. He'll get depressed." A beat, and then we all laugh. "But you know what I mean, don't you?" she asks.

"Okay," I say. "We won't ask about this one. We'll find another one. Let's go. You must be tired, anyway."

When we are in the car, Ruth says, "I'm actually not tired. I feel so good today. I don't have any of that back pain, I can breathe better. I have energy. Why are we looking at graves?"

No one answers.

When I get home, I sit in the wing chair by the bay window in the living room, feel my things around me like a blanket. I will make a fire, play music, read magazines with the afghan over my legs. When Meggie comes home from school, we'll play a game, or go shopping. I need time away from Ruth. There's nothing wrong with that. Anyone would need a break. I call my husband at work, tell him we're all going out to dinner and a movie tonight. "I want you to know I really appreciate how much you've been doing," I tell him.

"It's okay. It hasn't been so bad."

I pause, then ask, "Are you going to come and see Ruth, ever?"

"I don't know. Do you think I should?"

"She wants you to. And maybe you should pretty soon."

Silence.

"You know what I mean?"

"Yeah."

"Are you scared to go?" I ask.

A pause, and then, "I think so."

"It's okay," I say. "We're all scared. I mean, it's scary." I mean to laugh, but I start to cry.

"Maybe," he says, his voice gentle, "you need a few days away from her, huh?"

I nod, gulping, then say, "Yeah, that's what I decided, too. It's been kind of hard, sometimes."

"I know. I know it has. So let's just go out and try . . . well, don't take this wrong, okay? But let's try not to think about her."

"Okay. Okay. You're right. I know what you mean."

I hang up the phone. Then I go upstairs and lie down on Meggie's bed, find her scent in her pillow and push my face into it. I want everything that's mine to come to me right now. I want something inside me to get so full it pushes everything else away. There are other people who can be with her. I need a break. I tell myself this over and over, like a mantra.

Later, I call Ruth, tell her I won't be over that night. "Okay," she says. "That's fine. Helen's coming. Probably L.D., too."

"I just need to spend some time with Meggie and Joe," I say.

"Of course you do. I understand."

"You don't need me."

"No."

"I'll call you tomorrow."

"Okay."

We hang up and I immediately call her back. "I'll be there after the movie."

"Okay. Bring hot fudge."

It was around three years after we met that Ruth called at seven-thirty one morning and told me to come to the Gem Café. The Gem was our favorite. We liked the fact that there were stools at the counter and booths along the walls, that the menu was written on the back of pizza boxes taped unevenly above the grill. We had the good fortune to be there one day when one of the boxes fell into the spaghetti sauce. Stuie, the owner/cook, just fished it out with a spatula, wiped it off, and stuck it back up again. Not that you could count on what was on the menu actually being available. Stuie was moody. Sometimes you'd say, "I'll have today's special," and he'd say, "Don't have it." One July day Ruth and I went there for lunch and found a sign taped to the locked door saying, CLOSED. TOO HOT. But there was a pleasant, worn-down feeling to the place, like a favorite chair. And all the food was wonderfully bad for you.

"I can't come right now," I told Ruth. "You know that. I have to get Meg ready for school."

"When does her bus come?"

"Eight o'clock."

"Okay, then meet me at 8:05, okay?"

"I'll get there as soon as I can. What's up, anyway, Ruth?"

"I'll tell you when I see you."

"Are you all right?"

She hung up.

I got Meg on the bus, brushed my teeth, washed my face, and drove to the café in my pajamas. No one would know—I slept in sweat outfits. Anyway, I was worried. Something had happened.

When I came in, I saw her at a booth reading the paper. I slid in opposite her. "What?" I asked, breathless.

She looked up, smiled. "Hey, baby. Want some pancakes? Blueberry today, served with nine sticks of butter." She gestured toward her own plate, empty except for an incriminating ring of yellow.

"Come on, Ruth."

She folded the paper. "I did it."

"What?"

"I told Eric I'm moving out."

I sat back, stunned.

"I did it!"

"Jesus."

"He's not in," Ruth said. "You'll have to talk to me."

"Well, are you . . . did you tell Michael?"

"Get some pancakes," she said. "I'm so happy. Everything's fine."

I ordered pancakes and some of Stuie's soulful coffee. Then, while I ate, Ruth told me what happened.

"I was sitting at the kitchen table yesterday eating a tuna sandwich," she said, "and Eric walked in. He'd forgotten something that morning, so he'd come home to get it. He was on the way out the door and I called his name and when he turned around, I said, 'I want a divorce.' And he stood there and looked at me. And I just . . . I was remembering everything he'd done that had hurt me so much. I mean things I never even told you about, Ann, ways he made fun of me, humiliated me, like the time I was pregnant and asked him to just once put his head on my stomach to hear the baby in there and what he said was, 'Jesus, even your legs are getting fat.' I remembered everything as though it were one single incident, you know what I mean? And I felt as if I were being carried along by this huge, righteous wave, and I just . . . said it. And it felt fine, Ann. It's the right thing to do.''

''What did he say?''

She smiled bitterly. ''He said, 'I'm in a hurry, Ruth. What's your problem?' ''

''Are you kidding?''

She shook her head.

''That's it?''

''That's it. I told him I wasn't kidding. I told him I was going out to see an apartment that day. And I'd be moving as soon as possible. And he left and I finished my sandwich, which I enjoyed quite a lot—I'd put green olives in, you should try that, Ann, chop some green olives up and put them in there—and then I went and rented the apartment.''

''But what did you tell Michael?''

''That was the most amazing thing. He came home from school and I sat on the sofa with him and took a big breath and told him that I'd decided I needed some time alone, that Daddy and I were having some problems, and I wanted time to think about what the best thing to do was. He was absolutely calm. He said he understood. I know he was a little sad, but he was mostly . . . I don't know, *prepared*, as if he'd just been waiting for this. I suppose he has been. Anyway, he knows the apartment is close enough to walk to, he knows he can stay with me whenever he wants, and he's all right! I can't believe I waited this long. I feel like a noose is off my neck. Wait till you see my place—it's so pretty. Of course, I'll have to get a real job now, I can't rely on what I make from painting.''

''This feels . . . there's something wrong here,'' I said.

''You think this is too easy.''

I nodded.

''You think I'm in some manic phase, that the truth will hit pretty soon.''

I shrugged, then nodded again. ''Yeah, I guess so. Something like that.''

''You know what's wrong here, Ann?''

''What?''

''You.''

———— ❧ ————

She was right. I just couldn't quite believe that everything was happening as smoothly as it was. Michael was fifteen now, caught in the bulldog jaws of adolescence. Surely this kind of change in his life would be extremely difficult for him; surely he would pay the highest price for Ruth's freedom. But I had dinner with her and Michael at her apartment soon afterward and saw nothing but a sweet and calm boy who openly loved his mother and had learned to make tacos. These he proudly served on orange and yellow paper plates, selected, he said, for "that fiesta feeling." He had Ruth's fine sense of humor: he'd strung jalapeño peppers on dental floss, made necklaces for us all to wear while we ate. There were no longing glances, no sighs, no leaks of sadness in his voice or in his face.

Finally, I did believe her. Michael *was* fine, and so was she, and, apparently, so was Eric. Two weeks after Ruth left, he began dating one of the paralegals he worked with. "She's a dweeb, Mom," Michael had told her. "She's never funny."

"Is she pretty?" Ruth asked, and Michael said, "Gag me, Mom. What a woofer. Red hair. *Freckles.*"

Ruth's apartment was small, but it was beautiful—high ceilings, lots of windows, a fireplace in both the bedroom and the living room. She lined up pieces of pottery on the mantles, hung her artwork above that. She painted her walls delicate shades of pastels: peaches; blues; pale, pale yellows. At a garage sale, she found an Oriental rug made only more elegant by its fading colors and thinning nap, and she put it on her living-room floor. She kept white birch logs in her fireplace, baskets of beautiful rocks and seashells on her coffee table. Birds' nests lodged above doorways, in corners on open kitchen shelves. At night, she burned candles, several of them grouped together like lit bouquets. I loved being in her apartment. As soon as you walked in the door, you relaxed. It was a woman's place, plainly and un-apologetically. It seemed to me to breathe, to wipe its hands on its apron and welcome you in, inquiring im-mediately as to your spiritual well-being.

She took a job at a software company, something in marketing. This meant that we could no longer spend long afternoons together, but we talked every day and saw each other at least one night a week. It was on one of those nights a full year later that she told me about her lump. "Come with me to get the biopsy," she said. "Maybe I'll feel weird after, and I won't want to drive." Then, looking at my french fries, she said, "Are you going to finish those?"

I pushed my plate toward her. "Aren't you scared?"

She waved her hand in dismissal. "I've got lumpy breasts. I've been through this before, no big whoop. Slice and dice, hardly a scar left behind. It's never been anything before. It won't be this time, either."

"Okay," I said.

She looked up. "It *won't* be!"

"Okay, I believe you! What time?"

"Nine-thirty," she said. "Want to go out and look at fabric afterward? I'm taking the whole day off."

"Of course," I said. Ruth and I could spend hours in a fabric store. She was the only woman I'd ever met whose fascination for those places matched mine. The colors. The quiet undercurrent of industry. The tactile pleasure and smells of jewel-colored silks, calico cottons, wide-wale corduroy, pristine interfacings. We enjoyed looking through pattern books, especially when they got old and you could feel the history of so many hands on them. We loved the racks of buttons, all with personalities: shy pearls, flamboyant rhinestones, sensible round navy-blue buttons, lined up three in a somber row—Ruth said if they were little girls they'd all go to Catholic school. Every time we went there we admired the expensive scissors kept behind a glass case, and one

Christmas I finally gave Ruth a pair. She made a house for those scissors—lined a drawer with burgundy velvet and kept nothing but them there. I was a novice at sewing and struggled through each thing I attempted. Ruth made a raincoat, fully lined suits with invisible zippers, slipcovers for her sofa out of gorgeous French florals whose very presence on their five-foot-long bolts intimidated me. When winter came, we built huge fires and spent hours piecing together quilts on her bedroom floor. The wind rattled her windows and occasionally, with thrilling gusts, pushed itself into the room with us. But we were warm and distracted, sitting in our turtlenecks and flannel shirts and sweatpants and thick socks. Our hair was secured up off our faces with chopsticks and we were listening to moody jazz on the radio, drinking cocoa, and making art that would last for years. We were protected.

Of course we didn't go to a fabric store that day. Because the lump was not nothing.

I was in the waiting room, watching television and reading magazines, looking at my watch with greater and greater frequency. It was taking too long. Finally, the surgeon came out and called my name. I followed him to a corner of the room. He began speaking, but he wouldn't look at me, and I felt every part of myself grow stiff and cold. "It's not good," he said and I began nodding like an idiot.

I stayed with her that night. Both of us crowded onto her little bed, like sisters. "Aren't you at all scared?" I asked, just before we fell asleep. She had reacted to her diagnosis as though she'd encountered a minor road detour. She hadn't wept. She hadn't looked anxiously about. Her hands stayed still, resting half open on her lap. Her only movement was to cross her legs and lean back in her chair. A moment passed. Then she sighed and said, "Shit." And then, leaning forward again, "So. How are we going to get rid of this?" The surgeon said she should come to his office in a few days and discuss it. Ruth looked at me and I nodded yes I would go with her.

"I know whatever happens, I'll get through this," she said that night. "I know I'll be fine. I just *know* it. Don't you feel that, sometimes, a kind of absolute sureness?" I could smell her shampoo, feel the slight pull her weight created on her side of the bed. I could see the dim outline of all her things around us, her furniture, the art on her walls, the restless flutter of her curtains in the night air. In her jewelry box, bracelets and earrings waited, in her cupboard were unopened cans of soup and boxes of spaghetti. Mail came addressed to her; her voice was on her answering machine; she had a savings account and a checking account and ice skates she used every winter. Where could danger fit in her busy life? I turned my pillow over, flipped my hair up to feel the coolness against my neck. I relaxed. Because I believed her.

"I guess I do have some real sureness about some things," I said. "I know I won't die on a plane. That's why I'm never afraid to fly."

Ruth yawned, then said, "How do you think we do know that stuff?"

"Grace," I said.

"What?"

"Grace. I mean, I think that's what grace is, the messages we get. Only we miss most of them."

"Grace is 'God's loving mercy toward mankind,' " Ruth said. "I learned it in Sunday school."

"Well, that's what I mean," I said. "They're merciful, those messages. If only we could understand them."

R uth wore a black knit dress to meet with the surgeon. I wore a purple sweater over my jeans, having heard that it was a healing color. I tried to tell Ruth to change when I picked her up.

"Why?" she asked.

"Well . . ."

She strode over to the full-length mirror in her bedroom. "Does this look bad? Is my stomach sticking out?"

"No. It's just grim, black. Funereal. It might bring bad luck."

"Oh, bullshit. I look fabulous. Let's go."

In the car, Ruth told me about having seen Eric the day before. "He came over and tried to offer his re-

78 grets, you know. I was actually sort of glad to see him. I was telling him about what the deal was, and I asked him if he wanted to see what they'd done, you know, the biopsy site? I don't know why. I think I just wanted to man-test it, see if the next time I sleep with someone they'll be freaked out about a scar on my boob. I mean, this one was a decent cut.''

"So what did he say about it?''

She laughed. "He didn't even look! I started to pull my shirt up and he said, 'Ruth, do you mind?' ''

"Good old Eric.''

She shrugged. "Maybe he's squeamish.''

"Maybe he's a jerk.''

When we arrived at the doctor's office, Ruth and I sat together on one side of a massive desk. The surgeon came in, unfamiliar-looking now in a dark-brown suit. He sat opposite us, folded his hands on top of the desk, raised his eyebrows. Then he sighed nearly imperceptibly.

Uh-oh, I thought.

"So,'' he said. "How are you, Ruth?''

She laughed.

He smiled, embarrassed, then said, "Has this . . . sunk in a little over the last few days?''

She shrugged. "Well, I guess so. I think it's just the suddenness that's the problem. I mean, I'm fine. I'm really healthy. I ran three miles the morning before you cut me. It's like you're doing dishes or something and the phone rings and somebody else answers it and hands it to you and says, 'It's for you. It's cancer.' ''

The doctor stared at her, attempted an empathetic nod.

"Of course, I know I'll be fine and everything; it's just kind of a shock, that's all. I woke up the past two mornings and thought, wait, what's wrong, something's wrong. And then I remembered."

He looked down at her file, pulled out a paper, cleared his throat. "We got the full path report back," he said.

Ruth opened her purse, got a stick of gum. "And?"

"Well. It's not too good, Ruth. What you have are the most aggressive kinds of cancer cells—highly undifferentiated. And of course, you're premenopausal."

"I certainly am," she said, nudging me with her elbow. She wasn't understanding. I thought I remembered that breast cancer acts worse when you're premenopausal. I stared straight ahead.

"You might want to consider a mastectomy," the doctor said. "Under these circumstances, most women do. The other choice would be a lumpectomy. Either choice will be followed, of course, by chemotherapy and radiation therapy. We'll need to check your nodes. That will be the best prognosticator. We'll hope it's not there. If it is . . . well, we'll cross that bridge when we come to it."

She sat quite still, then turned to me, held out her pack of gum. "Want a piece of this?"

I shook my head no.

"Take some," she said, and I did.

L.D. meets me at Ruth's door. "Did you bring it?" she asks.

"What?"

"Hot fudge."

I hold up the gigantic container.

"Wow. I didn't know you could buy that much."

"You can now."

"Let's go," she says, and starts for the kitchen. "Ruth's really hungry. She's eating like crazy." She turns around to look at me. "This is it. I think she's turned the corner. I swear to God. I think she's getting better. I'm bringing her some more of those Chinese pills. And we need to get her out more. She can make it. I know she can."

I wish I had L.D.'s unwavering hope. Sometimes I think I'm starting to get close to it, and then I remember standing beside Ruth only a couple of weeks ago while her doctor showed her her chest X rays, her CAT scan. We'd been taken to a little room with light boxes so we could see them, and her doctor was pointing out all the pathology. A radiology resident had been in the room when we came in, looking at Ruth's films, and his face changed from curiosity into something resembling fear mixed with pity when Ruth's doctor introduced her to him. The name on the films! Here! He actually stepped back after he said hello, as though she were contagious. I stepped closer to her, stared at him defiantly.

But after she shook his hand, Ruth ignored him, looked
instead at pictures of her own lungs.

"This," her doctor said, beginning his horrible
lecture, "is the cancer in your lungs, Ruth. This whiteness." He pointed here, there, everywhere. Then, de-
feated, he put his hand down at his side. "I mean . . .
it's just a snowstorm in there." He wasn't being cruel.
Ruth had insisted that she be shown these things. "I
want to see it," she said. "Then I can visualize it going
away."

Next her doctor showed her slices of her brain
from the CAT scan. "It's here," he said, pointing again.
"And here." Then, in a voice we could barely make
out, "And . . . here."

"Jesus," Ruth said.

"Yes," he said. "It's impressive." He was using
the vocabulary of medicine. He was hiding. He showed
her her liver, her besieged spine.

"So," Ruth said. "You're absolutely sure we
should stop the chemo? It won't help at all?"

He shook his head.

"Radiation?"

"No."

"Nothing, really *nothing* you can do, Howard?"

"I'm sorry."

She sighed, looked at the radiology resident, by
now skulking like a rat in the corner. Then she smiled at
me, oh, this radiant smile. "Want to go to the movies?" she asked.

We went. We found a comedy and we went. And
on the way there, Ruth said, "Now, don't think this is

crazy, okay? I'm actually sort of relieved. Now it's just up to me. It's all under my control. I always felt so helpless when they were giving me all that stuff. I mean, with the chemo, you know, I would watch it drip in and look around the room and read stupid magazines and I just felt . . . I don't know, it felt wrong. I was always real nervous. Scared to death. I couldn't do any of that visualization, couldn't see the chemo as this good, gold stuff that would save me. I never did, Ann, even when I told you I did. And when I got radiation and this huge machine was hanging over me and all the technicians had to leave the room and stare at me from the booth . . . I can't tell you what that feels like! You're so much at the mercy of someone else's idea! And these ridiculous posters on the wall, saying 'If life gives you lemons, make lemonade.' Please!! This way . . . I don't know, I've always worked best when I'm in charge. I'll eat a billion carrots. I'll work out my own way. Maybe I had to get this bad so I could take over and get better. Maybe.'' She looked out the window. ''I think maybe so.''

I said nothing. I found an illegal parking place close to the doors of the movie, the manager's spot, so she wouldn't have to walk so far. We saw a comedy and we laughed out loud, a lot. After the movie was over, we went to the bathroom and Ruth washed her face at the sink, then stood up and looked at herself in the mirror. ''For a dead guy, I look good as hell,'' she said.

She did all right for a while. Then she started getting weaker. But now L.D. swears she's getting better again. Maybe Ruth was right. Maybe she'll heal herself

in the nick of time and show up in all the medical jour-
nals.

I start to go to Ruth's room. I want to see her. I
want to see the evidence. I'm starting to get excited.
But L.D. stops me. "Just stay in here and help me make
sundaes," she said. "Fucking Eric is here."

"What for?" I ask.

"I don't know, exactly. Something about her will.
Something about money to be left for Michael."

"Oh."

L.D. hears the disappointment in my voice.
"Come on," she says, pulling the ice cream from the
freezer. "What did you think? That he came to bring
her roses, to tell her how wonderful she is?" She pulls
the lid off the ice cream, digs her fingers in, and puts a
big helping into her mouth. "Does she have any bana-
nas?" she asks. "Nuts?"

I get three bowls from the cupboard, set them on
the table. "I think we should wait a minute before we
make these, L.D. Wait till he leaves. I don't want to eat
in front of him."

She turns to look at me, surprised. "Why not?"

"I don't know. He's so . . ." I lower my voice.
"He makes me so uncomfortable. He'll probably tell
me I chew wrong."

"Let's go see if they're almost done," L.D. says.
Then, over her shoulder, "You worry too much about
other people, Ann. You're all the time worrying about
what other people think."

"I know."

"Cut it out."

"Okay."

The door to Ruth's bedroom is closed. L.D. starts to open it, then stops. They are arguing. Ruth's voice is distraught, saying she didn't know something, and then Eric's muffled voice is asking how could she not know, what kind of incompetent does she have handling her affairs anyway? I am astounded at the level of his insensitivity.

L.D. opens the door, and Ruth turns quickly toward her, red-eyed.

"Want some ice cream?" L.D. asks, her voice so smooth and low it gives me chills. I move in to stand close behind her.

"Oh, thanks, L.D.," Ruth says. "No, I don't think so. You guys go ahead. We're almost done."

"You wanted a hot fudge sundae," L.D. says, staring at Eric.

"I know," Ruth says. "But maybe later, okay?"

There is an awkward silence, and then Eric says, "You'll need, naturally, to take care of this right away, Ruth."

She nods, then flings the covers aside. "I have to pee." We hear her crying quietly after she closes the bathroom door. Eric crosses his legs, sighs, leans back in the chair. Then, when he looks at his watch, L.D. is on him. She grabs at his chest, picks up handfuls of his burgundy V-necked sweater and white shirt, leans in close to his face. "Time's up, pal."

Eric looks coldly into her face. "Let go of me."

"Oh, I don't think I should do *that*, Eric. Because if I let go of you, I'll punch your fucking face so fucking hard you'll end up on fucking Pluto. Now, get the fuck out of here.''

"So eloquently put," Eric says, and awkwardly rises. L.D. still has hold of him.

"L.D.," I whisper.

She turns to me, her eyes devillike slits. "What?"

"Well . . ." I gesture toward Eric. "Let him go."

She looks down at her hands, lets go. He straightens his sweater, rights his posture, reaches for a manila envelope on Ruth's bed. He starts toward the door, turns back to look at L.D. and me and shakes his head. Then he closes the door quietly behind him.

"I'm going to push him down those steps and break his goddamn head open," L.D. says quietly. "He's such a fucking asshole. He's just a goddamn asshole. He's really an asshole. The stupid fuck."

"But do you like him?" I ask.

Ruth comes out of the bathroom and we both turn quickly toward her. When she sees Eric gone, she looks questioningly at us. "He had to go," L.D. says.

Ruth nods, climbs into bed. "Oh. Okay."

"He had an appointment with the Marquis de Sade."

Ruth smiles. "Did you scare him away, L.D.?"

"Yes."

"Well. Good." She fluffs her pillows up behind her. "I think I'll have that sundae after all, okay?"

L.D. goes into the kitchen and I sit beside Ruth on the bed. "What did he want?"

"Oh, I've done something wrong in the will. I have to . . . I don't know. Sarah will help. It's okay. I

86 just have to make sure it gets done. As Eric reminded me, I don't have all the time in the world." She looks at me, smiles. "He's always been so very helpful."

"Where are the nuts?" L.D. yells.

"Right here," Ruth and I answer together. No matter what, neither of us can ever resist an easy opener. Ruth yells back that they are in the upper right-hand cabinet. Then, to me, she says, "You know what?"

"What?"

"I still don't have any of that pain. Until Eric got here, I was feeling really good. Why do you think that is? Do you think my brain's just not getting pain messages anymore or something?"

"I don't know."

She takes in a breath, looks hard at me. "Do you think I could be getting better?"

"I don't know."

"Oh, Ann, what if I were?"

"Well, that would be wonderful." I hold her tight against me, and say, "I'm so glad I'm here. I want you to know I am exactly where I want to be. I'm so happy to be with you. I don't want to be anywhere else. I don't want to be anywhere but here."

"Ann?"

"Yes?"

Anything. I will do anything for her. I hold her a little tighter.

"Will you make sure I get a lot of ice cream?"

L.D. kicks the door open, sees us embracing. "Break it up. Look what I got." She is holding a tray

with three bowls. There are towers of whipped cream
over what I know are at least five scoops of ice cream.

"Oh," Ruth says. "Never mind."

There is a knock, then Sarah's voice calling out
"Hello?"

"Here we go again," L.D. sighs.

"What we need," Ruth says, "is a *real* party."

"You want one?" I ask.

Ruth thinks about it, nods. "Yeah."

"Done," I say.

Sarah comes into the room, unwraps the scarf
from around her neck, unbuttons her coat. "I just
passed fucking Eric on the road. What an asshole."

L.D. raises her eyebrows, looks Sarah up and
down. Then, "Here," she says, handing Sarah her sundae. "I'll go make me another one."

It was shortly after Ruth had gotten her apartment
that she talked me into taking a trip with her to New
York City. I'd been there and hated it, and Ruth insisted that was because I'd seen it with the wrong person, namely, my husband. "Come with me," she said.
"Just for a weekend. I promise you'll love it."

I said I'd go mostly because I was in another marriage rut and the idea of a weekend without Joe seemed
like good medicine. Lately we couldn't have a conversation without it degenerating into a fight. "Did you pick
up the cleaning?" I'd ask, and he'd say, "What the hell
is that supposed to mean?" I'd begun to hate the sound

of his chewing, the sight of his shoes, one lying over the other in the corner of the bedroom. I separated them with disgust, as though I'd caught them messily mating, flung them hard into the back of his closet. I resented his shaver next to the bathroom sink; I wanted a bouquet of pansies there, I wanted a clear Lucite container holding all my makeup. I had recently had the bizarre experience of picking up the water glass he left in the sink and squeezing it with a shaking hand, making some sort of growling noise at it before I slammed it down hard in the dishwasher. I knew that Ruth didn't have to even look when she pulled something to drink out of her refrigerator—she'd picked everything for herself, so how could she not like it? All the mail she got was for her; each time the phone rang, that was for her, too. She could leave the light on to read until late into the night, or she could turn it off early and go to sleep without explanation. She could have terrific sex whenever she felt like it simply by picking up the phone. It was order-in service of inestimable quality. I muttered out loud to myself while I transferred loads of laundry from the washer to the dryer; I took aspirin for headaches; I sat at stop lights and wiped away tears that came more from anger than sorrow.

Shortly before Ruth suggested our trip, we had seen a movie with a fleshy scene that made my pelvis feel as if it was being pulled forward off my seat, and I heard a little groan come out of me that was absolutely involuntary. I blushed, snuck a look at Ruth to see if she'd noticed. She was staring straight ahead, seemingly oblivious, but then quietly asked, "Enjoying the show?"

Afterward, we walked slowly through the parking

lot toward our cars. The stars were so clear and beautiful I felt rebuked. I stopped to stare up at them and said, "Well, here I go, home to my lover. The man whose idea of foreplay is the eleven o'clock news."

"I'm so happy to go home alone," Ruth said. "I can call someone to come over, or I can get into my bed with my book. And most of the time, I like the book better. I'm finding out that I love being without a man."

"I know," I said, as though I did. Of course I didn't. I only imagined what her life was like, and then I imagined what my life would be like without Joe. It seemed clean and appealing, brave and correct. It seemed something I should work toward. Recently I'd actually had a conversation with Meggie wherein I sat her on the sofa and said, "How would you like to live with just Mommy?"

"Yes!" she said. "And Daddy, too."

"No," I'd said, carefully. "I mean, what if you just lived with Mommy? And Daddy lived somewhere else?"

"No!" Her face screwed up, tears came to her eyes. I had two simultaneous impulses, both of them terrible: I wanted to slap her. And I wanted to put my head in her lap, say, "Oh Meggie, Meggie, please don't make me stay here." What I did was say, "Oh, come on. I'm just teasing you. Want to color?"

She shook her head, her mouth still trembling.

"Want to play Barbies?"

She shrugged, a victor intent on prolonging the victory. But then she went to her room and brought down her doll case, solemnly handed me the single,

90 naked Ken while she lined up the many Barbies. "What should they do?" she asked.

"I don't know," I'd sighed. "You decide."

So I watched Ruth drive away from the movie theater that night, looking at her straight neck as she sat behind the wheel, hearing the faint sound of James Brown's "I Feel Good" coming from her tape player, and I had a nearly irresistible urge to follow her. "Move over," I would say, when I climbed into bed with her. "Let's have some cheese and crackers while we read. I'm staying." I had to sit still for a long time that night before I headed in the other direction.

On the plane to New York, Ruth pointed out the window. "Look how beautiful everything is down there," she said. "How can you see that and believe there is trouble in the world?"

I leaned past her to look outside. It was nighttime, and the lights below were like jewelry thrown randomly down on black velvet. I liked imagining someone in a kitchen below us peeling potatoes for dinner, having no idea that their overhead light was making such a spectacular contribution. Cars moved toylike along the highways, their headlights peaceful and straight before them.

"Do you want to trade now?" Ruth asked. We'd agreed to switch seats halfway, after discovering we both liked to sit by the window. But now I shook my

head no. I was feeling irritated, and didn't want to im-
prove my mood until I found out what was wrong.

"Get the waitress, will you?" Ruth asked. "I
want another drink."

"She's not a waitress," I said. "She is a flight attendant. She is here primarily for your safety. But if
there's anything she can do to make your flight more en-
joyable, please don't hesitate to call on her."

"She's a waitress," Ruth said. "And she's here
primarily for our drinking pleasure. And to give us
sandwichettes that taste like nothing, even when you
put mustard on them."

True. Our snacks lay mostly untouched on our
tray tables, covered with napkins like a shroud. The
flight attendant walked past and I said, "Miss? Could we
get another drink, here?"

"Sure can," she said, in the smoothly nonjudg-
mental voice of the airline professional. Then, pointing
to our tray tables, "All through with your snacks?"

Ruth snorted. "Well, I guess so!"

After the attendant left, I told her, "You know,
sometimes you are just too mean to people!"

"What are you talking about?" she asked, and
then, whispering, "She's not a person; she's a flight attendant. They're blow-up dolls."

"I mean it," I said.

Her face became serious and she said, "I know. I
know I do that. I'm sorry."

"Don't tell *me*," I said. "I'm not the one you
should apologize to."

When she was brought her drink, Ruth reached

92 out toward the flight attendant and said in a low voice, "I'm sorry."

"Pardon?" The woman half smiled. She was wearing pearl studs, and one of them hung endearingly loose on her lobe. I wanted to point to it and say to Ruth, "See? Don't you see how we all need each other?"

"I'm sorry I was rude to you," Ruth said.

Now the attendant smiled fully. "Oh, you weren't rude."

Ruth looked at me, smirked.

"Nobody likes the food."

"Well, I want you to know I appreciated the presentation," Ruth said. "You know. Curly lettuce and everything. That little radish cut into the shape of . . . whatever it was."

The attendant shrugged. "I'm not the chef."

"Were you ever in a wreck?" Ruth asked, and the flight attendant said no and left.

"You drink too much, too," I said.

"Are you crabby because you didn't get the window seat?" Ruth asked.

"No. Yes."

"Well, trade then."

"No."

Ruth sipped her drink, stretched out her legs. "We're almost there. Relax. Stop feeling so guilty. It's only a weekend."

"I'm not guilty!" I said.

She waved her hand. "Oh, please! Not much!"

"Well, aren't you?"

"No!"

"Why not?"

"Why should I be?"

"I don't know. Because of Michael."

"He's with his dad. And Meg is with *her* dad. They're fine. And we're fine." She yawned, stretched. "I got us dates for dinner."

"What?"

"You'll have fun. You don't have to fuck anyone. Although you can."

"I shouldn't have come," I said.

"You're finally beginning to be happy that you did," Ruth said. I said nothing until she asked, "Aren't you?" and then I nodded. And then I got my own drink. A blind date, I was thinking. I hadn't had one of those since I didn't know what age spots were.

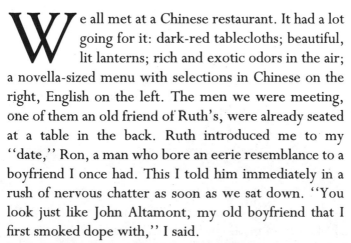

We all met at a Chinese restaurant. It had a lot going for it: dark-red tablecloths; beautiful, lit lanterns; rich and exotic odors in the air; a novella-sized menu with selections in Chinese on the right, English on the left. The men we were meeting, one of them an old friend of Ruth's, were already seated at a table in the back. Ruth introduced me to my "date," Ron, a man who bore an eerie resemblance to a boyfriend I once had. This I told him immediately in a rush of nervous chatter as soon as we sat down. "You look just like John Altamont, my old boyfriend that I first smoked dope with," I said.

Ruth smiled, pulled her chair closer to her man for

the evening, a smallish type named Dennis wearing a black turtleneck sweater and John Lennon glasses, so handsome that if he weren't petite he would be irritating. She put her arm around him and said, ''We did that for the first time together too, remember?''

Dennis smiled, nodded. ''Yeah, that's what I told you.''

Ruth took her arm away and sat back, surprised. ''You weren't a dope virgin?''

He shook his head. ''I had thirty cubes of acid in my backpack that night. After I left your house, I went out and took one and sold the rest.''

''My, my. The things you don't know about a person,'' Ruth said.

''The things you can learn,'' Ron said. And then, leaning closely in toward me, ''Such as . . . what exactly do *you* like?'' He picked up the menu, to protect himself with a certain ambiguity.

''I don't remember,'' I said.

''Been a long time since you've, uh . . . had Chinese?'' he asked.

''It's been a very long time.''

He waited. I crossed my legs, swung my foot a little. ''Tell you what,'' I said. ''I'm going to point to something on the Chinese side, and then I'm going to eat it, no matter what it is. I need a new experience.'' I held my face in a way I hoped made my cheekbones prominent.

''Delivery man,'' Ron said, in an oily voice. Then he licked his lips. I uncrossed my legs, ordered garlic chicken from the English side, requested a fork to eat it with. Something had evaporated, almost instantly. That's what I told Ruth when we got back to our hotel.

She nodded. "Bad feet syndrome, huh?"

"What do you mean?"

"Oh, you know, you're thinking maybe you'll go ahead and do it and then they take their socks off and their toes are weird and you don't want to anymore."

"Something like that. Actually, I think I just all of a sudden remembered . . . I don't know, who I am, I guess." I felt an annoying urge to apologize.

"Well, too bad. I'd have done it if you had. We could have invited them here. Stereo sex."

"Are you kidding?" I asked.

"No." She pulled her jeans off, her sweater. She wasn't wearing a bra and I saw her breasts for the first time, which were perfect: nice size, pert pink nipples, pointed slightly upward. She pulled her nightgown over her head, shook her long hair loose from the tie she'd had it up in.

"Jesus!" The word sort of exploded out of me.

"What?" She stretched out on her bed, put the pillow over her stomach.

"Well, you can't just go around fucking everybody! I mean, it's . . . passé, even!"

"I'm not interested in fucking everybody. Only some people."

"I didn't come all the way to New York to lay some guy I never met. I want to be boring. I want to go to the museums. I want to eat one of those hot dogs from the cart. I want to go to Tiffany's and try on a diamond bracelet."

"Tomorrow," Ruth said. "All this and more."

"Fine."

We turned out the lights, listened to the vaguely distressing sounds of sirens in the distance. "We're in New York City," I said.

"Um-hum."

"Everything is so . . . busy. You feel as if you have to quick hurry up and say things to people, like they're tapping their foot, can't wait to get on to the next thing. Everybody's like that!"

"Yes."

"Doesn't it make you nervous?"

"No."

"It's too much, here. I mean, I'm having fun and everything, but it's too *much*. Just walking down the block is so . . . *intense*. And everybody acts like it's normal!"

"It is normal, here."

I pulled the covers higher over me. "Are you going to call home?"

"You can call home if you want to."

I thought about it. But the truth was, I didn't want to. I wanted to think about what it would be like to live in New York City. Maybe I could have had some cramped but arty apartment, walked to my exotic job every day wearing big sunglasses and weird shoes, never married, opened cans of tuna for six or seven cats every night. Why does what happens in our lives, happen? Who really decides?

"You know, my grandmother was a real wild woman," I told Ruth.

"Really?"

"Yeah. Rumor has it that she was pregnant before she got married."

"Was it the father she married?"

"Well, of course!"

Ruth laughed. "It does happen that sometimes the mother marries someone else."

I waited a moment, then asked, "Is that what you did?"

Silence. I strained to see her in the dark, but I couldn't. They make hotel curtains to serve well in a blackout.

"Ruth?"

"I don't know," she said. "It could have been Eric's baby. It could have been someone else's."

"*Whose?*"

"This other guy. I really loved him, but he wasn't the marrying kind."

"Neither are you," I said.

"I could have been," she said.

"Jesus, Ruth. Did Eric know?"

"No."

"He just thought you got pregnant right away?"

"Right."

"Was Michael 'premature?' "

"Of course. By six weeks."

"And Eric didn't suspect anything?"

"No. I'm tired. I'm drunk. Let's go to sleep."

I stayed awake. I stared up at the ceiling, thinking, how can I love a woman I basically disapprove of? And then, the aftershock, how can I love a woman?

We are in the kitchen—L.D., Sarah, Helen and I—planning Ruth's party. "Who else?" I ask, chewing on the pencil I'm using for the guest list. We have thought of fifteen women so far. "Should we do guys?"

"No," L.D. says. It is an autonomic reflex for her, like breathing. She doesn't even look up.

"Ruth *likes* some guys," I say.

"Yeah," Helen says. "What about those two guys she goes to hear music with at that country-and-western bar?"

"Tim," I say. "And . . ."

"I think it's Luther," Helen says.

"Tim and *Lu*ther?" L.D. asks.

"It's not his fault," Sarah says. "His parents named him."

"No guys," L.D. says.

The phone rings, and I answer it on the first ring. Ruth is sleeping; I don't want it to wake her up. I say "Hello" softly into the receiver. It is Ruth's brother, Andrew, calling from Florida, to see how she is.

"Well . . . actually, better," I say.

"Really?"

"She's had a good few days. No pain. And she's eating real well."

"Is she going out at all?"

"Not a lot. She hasn't been out a lot lately. You

know what we're doing now, though? Planning a party
for her!''

Silence.

"I mean, not a party, really. But, well, yes, maybe it is a party. Sort of.''

Silence.

"She, you know, asked for one.''

An even breath in, and then her brother says, "Uh-huh. Well, I'm wondering if she ought to come here, now.''

"I don't think so.''

"I know she's told you she doesn't want to, but I'm wondering if it wouldn't be best at this point. I mean, considering her prognosis. I spoke to her doctor this morning. It sure doesn't look good. And I am her only family.'' He says the word as though it's a placard he's carrying.

"Look,'' I said. "She has told me she wants to stay here, even when . . . no matter what happens. She's told me that more than once, Andrew.'' I can feel heat rising up into my face. I look toward the kitchen. Usually Sarah handles this kind of thing. She is all gentle diplomacy, but her face stays full of nonnegotiable intent, her gaze clear and steady. Ruth told me she knows how to use body language to her advantage: at a critical moment in a meeting, she will simply get up, cross the room on her Joan-and-David heels and stand before her opponent, still talking in her soft voice, and she will win, because the person can't look up at her and feel that he has any authority. "It's like all of a sudden they're in their bathrobes, with bed head,'' Ruth said.

On the phone with Andrew, Sarah's manner is so cool and decisive it forbids conflict. I'll never be able to handle myself the way Sarah does. It requires a certain maturation I don't expect to ever achieve. Every time Andrew has tried to persuade (bully, L.D. says) Ruth into coming to his house for "final care," as he calls it, Sarah has always taken the phone and told him to fuck himself. In a very nice way.

"She does have the right to change her mind," Andrew says now.

"And if she does I'm sure she'll tell you." I realize my voice has gotten loud, and I return to a quieter one, saying, "We're taking good care of her, you know. Someone's with her all the time."

"I know that," he says, and I suddenly have an image of him staring out his window, seeing a Christmas morning when he and Ruth sat cross-legged in their pajamas, ripping open presents. I see his hand go deep into his pocket, seeking the comfort of spare change.

"I mean, this party thing," I say. "She really did suggest it. I think the notion of a lot of her friends around—"

Ruth is up out of bed and standing at the entrance to her living room. "Who's that?" she asks, rubbing one eye.

"Your brother." I hand her the phone.

"Andy-man," she says, sitting down and drawing her flannel shirt around her tighter. It's a deep-blue plaid, makes her eyes stand up and salute. "Hi, sweetie, how are you?"

A long pause. I go back into the kitchen, put my finger to my lips, sit at the table and eavesdrop with all my might. As does everyone else. Helen's teacup is in midair.

"Oh, no," we hear her saying. "No, I don't think I want to, Andy."

Long pause.

"I know you do, I know you would. But I want to stay here."

Longer pause, then Ruth's voice, hesitant, "Yes, I have thought about that. But they're taking good care of me. I'm all right."

"Goddamn him," L.D. says.

"Shhhh!" the rest of us say.

But Ruth is talking too low for us now, and she does, after all, deserve some privacy in her own house. We return to the guest list. "So. No guys, right?" L.D. says. The air has changed, and, like oath takers, together the rest of us solemnly answer, "Right."

When Ruth is off the phone, she comes into the kitchen. The phone rings again. She sighs, asks L.D. to get it for her.

"It's Joel somebody," L.D. says. "Do you want to talk?"

Ruth sucks in a breath, lays a hand across her chest. "Joel? Really? Joel *Fratto*?"

L.D. shrugs.

Ruth goes into the living room, and we hear her say, "Is this Joel Fratto?" Then she nearly yells, "No! No! I don't believe this! How did you find me?"

"Who's that?" Sarah asks.

I don't know, and neither does L.D., but Helen says, "That's her old boyfriend, the one she had before she married Shithead."

"The artist?" I ask.

Helen nods. "He was really handsome. She's got a picture somewhere. He's on a motorcycle, with no shirt."

I feel a blip of jealousy—I've never seen that picture.

"I wonder why he's calling," I say. "Do you think he knows?"

Ruth comes into the kitchen, flushed and wide-eyed. "He's coming over here," she says. "I've got a fucking *date!*"

"Who is this guy?" L.D. asks.

Sarah stands up to give Ruth her chair. "Are you sure you feel okay to see him?"

Ruth pushes a pile of insurance forms on the kitchen table out of the way, sits there. "This is the fourth day in a row I've felt absolutely fine," she says. "God, Joel Fratto!"

"What the hell kind of name is that?" L.D. asks.

"He was so wonderful," Ruth answers.

"What about this party, Ruth?" L.D. wants to know. "Do you still want a party? I think we should talk about that."

"I still want everything," Ruth says. "I just remembered. I still do. Where's my wig? Where's my boobs? Help me. I want to do my eyes, too."

L.D. is frowning, Sarah looks a little worried, Helen is beaming, and I'm confused. We've been talking codicils. We've been visiting graveyards. Now we've got to find Ruth's mascara so she can get ready for a date.

She goes into the bathroom to fill up the tub, and

Helen and Sarah follow her, suggesting things they can
do to help. Their sounds are soft and overlapping and
full of a kind of subdued cheerfulness, like birds before
they go to sleep. L.D. and I are sitting at the kitchen
table, immobilized by irritation and astonishment re-
spectively. L.D. tips her chair back on two legs, puts
her hands behind her head. "Well. Maybe we should go
buy her some protection. I saw some condoms in the
drugstore the other day with fireworks on the box."
She moves a toothpick she's been chewing on to the
other side of her mouth, raises her eyebrows up and
down.

"Is this . . . real?" I ask.

She shrugs. "What the hell difference does that
make?"

———— ❧ ————

Once, a couple of years after Ruth had moved
out, she went out of town to visit a friend,
and I stayed in her apartment for a night. I
told Joe it was to keep an eye on things, but I think he
knew I wanted to try it on.

At first, I loved it. I changed into one of Ruth's
beautiful silk robes, so smooth against my skin I could
barely feel it. Then I turned the radio on to a classical
station and made dinner for myself in her little blue-
and-white kitchen—breast of chicken and mushrooms
in white wine sauce, wild rice, green beans—all cooked
in copper pans. For dessert I had a huge piece of apple
pie with ice cream, eaten off a pottery plate. It was so

pretty I had to keep picking it up to inspect it from all angles while I ate.

Then I walked around looking at things. It was so calm, her apartment, so carefully thought out. I examined the artwork on the walls: watercolors of nasturtiums on a windowsill and one of a turtle, head raised expectantly and eyes revealing a kind of patient wisdom. On the bedroom wall was a large print that showed a group of women sleeping outside in a field, some of them with the tops of their dresses loosened to reveal their cleanly white breasts, their soft stomachs. Some of the women lay flat; some were on their sides, and their arms made pillows for themselves or hung relaxed at their sides, and their hands were idle and defenseless and beautiful. Looking at that print, you could feel the warmth of the pale-yellow sun on bare shoulders, you could smell the grass, you could know the exquisite relief of the passing breezes and the presence of other women who lay down with you. I knew that print was Ruth's favorite, and it was mine, too. Once, when we were looking at it together, I said, "How can they do that? Don't they have to go to the grocery store and get stuff for dinner?"

"They feed each other," Ruth said. "They don't need a thing."

I turned on the television, then turned it off. I looked through the stack of tapes by the stereo: Mozart. George Strait. Glenn Gould and Glen Miller. The Rolling Stones. In the bathroom, I looked in the medicine chest and saw a neat line of aspirin and Tylenol and cough syrup. There was a box of invisible Band-Aids and a nail clipper and a prescription bottle half full of diuretics. What was that for, I wondered. Weight loss? Could she be so silly?

There were several boxes of bubble bath on a shelf over the tub, and I picked one up to use, but found it empty. All of the others were too, all but one, which I suddenly felt I couldn't use. It was an illusion of riches, all those boxes. I couldn't take from her when in truth she had so little. I made my luxury be the hotness of the water, the depth of it.

When I had finished bathing, I went back into her bedroom and stood in the center of the room for a while, looking out the window, watching the clouds move across a full moon. There was the faint sound of someone on the phone next door, and nothing else. It was distressingly quiet in that apartment. Even the music I'd put on the radio seemed unable to penetrate a kind of bubble that had formed around me.

I opened Ruth's top dresser drawer. I felt guilty looking in it, but I suddenly needed to know something, though I didn't know what. Ruth's socks were rolled up and organized according to color. She had underpants stacked up in two piles, one pair directly on top of the other. There was a stack of the tiny cotton T-shirts she wore, folded precisely into fours. I thought, why are these like this? Who has time to do this? And then I realized that what I was seeing was not an obsessive kind of neatness, but loneliness. I got dressed, dried and put away the dishes I'd washed after dinner, and then I went home.

Later that night, I lay beside Joe as he watched the news. We didn't talk. But I knew everything had changed. I believe he knew, too.

Not long afterward, on a bright spring day when Ruth and I were sitting out on her balcony, she said, "I've been living here for two years now." Then, rather suddenly, "I want to go home."

"You want to go home?" I asked. "Is that what you said?"

She nodded, staring straight ahead.

"To Eric, you mean?"

"Well, to Michael mostly, I think is what it is. You know, I miss making him breakfast, giving him snacks after school. I'm beside myself when he's sick. Last time he had the flu, I called him a million times. I kept waking him up."

"Maybe he should live with you."

"I can't afford a big enough place. And anyway, it's more than that. I want . . . I miss the routine of three people, you know? Do you know how pathetic it is to do laundry for one? I used to think laundromats were interesting, even romantic. But now I think they're only filthy."

"Well," I said. "I don't know what to say. Michael will be going to college next year. And think of what Eric was like, really. Do you want that again?"

"He was good when I was sick. I never told you that. He brought me little flowers on my bed tray. And I . . . he wasn't the only one at fault."

"I know. I know that."

"I want to go home," she said again, her voice

simultaneously determined and beaten. "I don't like living alone. I needed to live alone to find that out. Funny, huh?" She stood, walked over to the edge of her balcony and I had a crazy thought that she might jump.

"Maybe you should talk to Eric," I said. "Tell him."

"I did." She leaned far over the balcony, and I started to get up, then stopped. "I put on some makeup and some great underwear and I went to see him and said I was sorry, that I thought I'd made a huge mistake and I wanted to try again. I said I understood a lot about what went wrong, that I thought we could fix it. I said we could learn to give each other happiness, that I'd come back next weekend, how about that, and I told him what I wanted to make for dinner that night. I even said we could go out and buy some new sheets together, to get *ready,* you know."

"Well," I sighed. "I'll miss this place. It's so pretty. I love to come here."

She straightened up, turned around to face me. "Oh, I'm not going back. He has a girlfriend. The paralegal he's been dating. He said they're 'informally engaged.'"

"What? Are you kidding?"

"Nope."

"Does Michael know?"

"Not yet. When they tell him, it'll be formal. They were thinking they'd wait till this summer, when Michael graduates. Then he can have time to think about things, spend some time with both of them together. He can get to know her real well, so they can be pals." She sat down in her chair, leaned back and closed

108 her eyes, pointed her chin toward the sun. "I think she's about twelve years old. Gonna start her period any day now."

"My God," I said. "I had no idea."

"Me neither. Obviously."

I sighed hugely, then asked, "Well, what's her stupid name?"

Ruth opened her eyes, turned to look at me. "*Jani*. With an *i*."

"Give me a break."

"That's what *I* said." Ruth smiled. "And you know what Eric said? He said, 'I won't tolerate your insulting her.' "

"Fuck him."

"I suggested that," Ruth said. "He declined. He feels nothing for me anymore. Before, even when he was terrible to me, at least there was . . . something. Even if it was only anger. Now there's this sort of . . . I don't know, impatient tolerance. I think he only talks to me at all because of Michael."

"Listen," I said. "You've been through so much lately. You got told you have cancer; they stole your breasts, you went through chemotherapy and radiation therapy. . . . Don't you think your wanting to go home is just a move toward some false sense of security?"

"What do you mean?"

"I mean you didn't get cancer till you left him. You want to be back there because that was the place where you didn't have it. You just want to feel safe."

She stared at me. "What's wrong with that? Wouldn't you?"

"I don't know," I said. "I really don't. You

know, in spite of everything you've gone through, I still envy you."

"Well, isn't that ironic?" she said, and I saw her suddenly in my chair at the dinner table, bathing Meggie, making love to Joe.

"I liked it better when you didn't need men," I told her.

She sighed. "I can't keep living out your fantasies for you forever. I'm tired. I wish I'd never left. You know, I write all the time in my journal about being home. I try to re-create scenes of my life back there just so I don't forget, and so I can have them again, just the ordinary stuff, just the regular routine I had, morning coffee in my blue cup, the ten-thirty mail, looking at Michael asleep every night before I went to bed. Smells in that house, even—the hallway always smelled like ironed clothes, remember? The living-room floor dipped in certain places, but you could only feel it in the summer, when your feet were bare. I remember the exact order of the canned soup in the cupboard, and then I think, well, it's probably been changed now, and that terrifies me. I want to go home. I just want to go home. Can't you understand that?" Her eyes filled, and she pushed the heels of her hands into them, then bent over, bowed by the kind of grief that will not let you stand straight.

I didn't say anything. I got out of my chair to put my arms around her, because I'd been so wrong about her, because I knew as well as she did that she'd never be able to go home again, and I was so sorry.

Things got worse. Ruth stopped going out. She wouldn't let me come over, would only talk to me on the phone. And then one night she called while I was eating dinner. I sat on the steps in the hall with the kitchen phone cord stretched taut and heard her say, "I have some pills here, Ann."

"What do you mean?" I asked.

She breathed out heavily.

"Ruth?"

"I don't want to be alive anymore. I don't, Ann. I'm miserable. I don't see anything changing. I don't have any hope. I want to stop. But I don't want Michael to know I did this. Help me figure something out."

"I'm coming over there," I said, and heard Meggie say, "Where's Mommy going? We're *eating*!"

"Don't come," Ruth said.

I went. I packed a bag for her, told her she was not safe alone and I was taking her to a hospital. They admitted her to the psych unit, and I left her sitting at the edge of a narrow bed, her hands folded on her lap.

For a week, I wasn't allowed to even talk to her. Then, when they told me I could visit, I went to the hospital and found her outside the main door, waiting for me. "I get to go out," she said. "Yahoo. Let's go get ice cream."

We went to a Friendly's and ordered gigantic sundaes. Her eyes were no longer flat; she'd moved back inside herself.

"They want me to go to AA meetings," she told me. "Can you believe that?"

I said nothing.

"I mean, I know I drink too much."

I shrugged.

"Do you think I drink too much?"

I meant to say, gently, that yes, she did, but what I did instead was to start crying, embarrassing myself. I thought it was because when I'd looked up to answer her, I'd seen the plastic hospital bracelet on her wrist, with its mean metal clasp, with its smeared and indifferent THOMAS, RUTH, but it wasn't that. It was that I loved her and realized at that moment that if she hadn't called me, I might have lost her. This I muttered, more or less, between the hands I held over my face.

"Hey," she said, moving out of her side of the booth to come and sit with me. "Hey. You're supposed to be taking care of me. You're supposed to be making sure I don't do crazy-person stuff. Stop crying."

"I'm so happy you didn't do it," I said. "I want you to always be here. You're my best friend. I never had one. Not like you."

"Will you stop crying?" she said. "Listen to me. I'll tell you a story. There's a guy in with me there, we play pool. He has big tattoos, but I kind of like him. I like him. He writes me poems, and there are no grammatical errors. Last night, he painted my toenails for me. Red."

I stopped crying. "Really?"

She nodded. "Don't get too excited. You have to do therapy shit all day. It's enough to drive you crazy, in case you're not already. Yesterday, we had to put our

112   chairs in a circle and we all were given colored scarfs, and we had to fling them into the air in front of us while we said, 'I'm *throw*ing my guilt away! I'm throwing my *guilt* away!'"

"God," I said, sniffing away the last of my emotional squall. "Well, when do you get to come home?"

"After I go to a couple of AA meetings, for one thing. Can you imagine? I *have* to go!"

"So go."

"Oh, it's a bunch of crap. A bunch of people sitting around in church basements, wearing polyester and drinking bad coffee out of Styrofoam cups. Smoking their brains out because they can't drink. And praying or something. I've heard about those things. They're not for me."

"Go anyway."

She sighed. "I will."

"Want me to come with you?" I asked.

"Yeah. We can go get drunk afterward."

"Go alone," I said. "I can see you need to go alone."

And she said, "I know. I will."

She did go, several times, and soon after that she came home. Three days after that, Eric married Jani with an *i*. I stayed with Ruth that whole day and night. We made a devil's food cake for breakfast and then we went and bought kites and found a park to fly them in and then we went to a movie and then we went out for a lobster dinner and then we went to another movie. After she got home, we played some Billie Holiday and it was only then that she cried for a while. I asked if she wanted to call the happy couple on their wedding night, see how Eric was making out with his premature ejaculation problem, and she said no, she thought half the reason she was crying was that she was relieved it was over.

She began rowing on the lake in the early morning for exercise, and lifting hand weights to rock and roll at night. She was going to concerts and plays with various men and movies with me, and she was saving money so that in a year she could buy a condo where Michael could stay with her when he was home from school. Then one day she came back from a follow-up chest X ray and called me on the phone and said, "Guess what? There's something on my lungs."

"It's probably nothing," I said. I was sitting at the kitchen table, doodling on a grocery list. "It's probably just a shadow." I stopped doodling, held still, waiting, until I heard her say, "Yeah. Probably."

Of course it was not a shadow. It was cancer, back and smiling. I lay in bed that night, weeping on Joe's chest. "Oh, it's so scary," I said. "I keep thinking, every time she breathes in, she must wonder, Is this making it worse? Am I hurting anything, moving these lungs in and out like this?"

Joe was pushing my hair back away from my forehead over and over, aching in his own way and for his own reasons. When Ruth had come over for the first time after her double mastectomy, he'd put down his sandwich, risen up from the kitchen table, kissed her, and told her she was the most beautiful woman he'd ever known.

"Well, *Joe,*" she'd said, looking over his shoulder at my face, tight with pride. And then she'd put her

114 arms around him and hugged him tight, then tighter, and then tighter still until he grunted in pain.

"This is a strong woman, here," she'd said. "Don't mess with me. Now that my tits aren't in the way, I can aim better."

"I thought she was cured," Joe said.

"I did, too," I said. "She did, too."

Silence, and then Joe said, "Who's with her, now? Who's holding her?"

I opened my eyes wide, stopped crying.

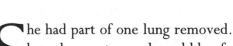

S he had part of one lung removed. I brought her a huge bouquet, purple and blue for healing, white because she loved white, and no carnations because she hated them. I gave her chest tube a name, Charles, because she was afraid of it. I held her hand when they pulled it. "Now," she said, after they'd put a dressing on. "Back to business. I'm really tired of these constant interruptions." She said something like that after she found out it was in her bones, too. Then, when it was in her brain, she quit saying it. When the work gets too hard, you stop talking about it. You just try to do it.

Ruth is wearing her wig, charcoal eyeliner, black mascara—"How *old* is this?" Helen asked, "I had to spit all over it to make it work!"—blush and lipstick. Her white silk blouse is tucked into her jeans, and she's put on her red ostrich-leather cowboy boots. She turns sideways before the mirror. "How do my falsies look?"

"Excellent," L.D. says. "You're definitely my kind of girl."

"Let me sit a minute," Ruth says, and squeezes between me and Sarah on her bed. Then, "Whew! I'm beat!" You can see her fatigue like a veil she is wearing, but, also like a veil, you can see her great beauty through it.

"If you're too tired, we can get rid of him," L.D. says. She is full of hope.

Ruth smiles. "No, I really want to see him. I want *you* guys to meet him. And then you have to leave for a while."

"What for?" I say.

The doorbell rings. We stand immobile, all of us, and then Ruth takes in a breath and gets up to answer it. Sarah straightens her bed while the rest of us wait nervously, picking at our nails or looking out the window, around the room. We hear Ruth say something, then a man's deep voice, then Ruth's laugh. L.D. sternly adjusts the bill of her hat so that it is centered over her forehead, then strides forth into the hallway to inspect him. Like ducklings, the rest of us line up and follow.

———— ❧ ————

H e still looks like a stupid movie star," Helen says. "I *hate* guys like that!"

"He brought her a rose," Sarah says. "He was nice. It was a good beginning."

L.D. snorts, finishes her beer. We are in a pizza parlor consoling ourselves, eating garlic bread and drinking beer—except for Helen, who has to go to work in a little while and has been told never to come to work after drinking again. ("The irony," she said, "is that I sold more books that night than I ever did. People trust drunks about art.")

"Well, I just want to know what this means," I say. "I thought . . . you know . . . I thought she was dying."

"She is dying," Sarah says. "Everybody always forgets that you die the way you live. She will keep on being herself until the end."

"What?" L.D. asks, her forehead wrinkled.

"You know, you stay the same person until the end."

"You think you know so much, Sarah," L.D. says, "just because of what you went through with your father. But that was one fucking death experience. You don't know everything. In addition to which maybe Ruth's not dying anymore. There are cases where people who are told they're terminal survive. They do a complete turnaround. They live. You might want to keep that in mind.''

''I know that happens,'' Sarah says, not unkindly. ''I also know that some things have got to be taken care of, in case it doesn't happen. Ruth asked me to help her do that. And I intend to.''

Helen and I look uneasily at each other. Then Helen pushes her chair back slightly, says, ''I think I know what's happening here. We're starting to take out on each other the fact that we've been dumped for a man.''

L.D. takes her toothpick out of her mouth, stares at her. ''We haven't been dumped. He's a visitor. He's not us.''

''*I* know,'' Helen says, though I wonder if she did know, before now.

''We've been here long enough,'' L.D. says, and signals the waitress for the check.

I don't want to leave yet. I want to talk some more about the possibility of Ruth not dying. But it's not the kind of thing to push too hard.

———— ❧ ————

H ow is she?'' Joe wants to know at supper that night.

''I don't know,'' I say. ''It's weird. She seems like she's getting better.''

''Who?'' Meggie asks. ''Ruth?''

''Yes.''

"She's better now?"

"I don't know," I say, with some irritation. "Eat your dinner."

"I didn't do anything," Meggie says.

"I didn't say you did."

"You're crabby," Meggie says, and I say I'm sorry.

On Saturday, I pick Helen up at the bookstore. We are going to Ruth's together. I arrive early, browse a little while I wait for Helen to get off. I like this bookstore. Scattered here and there are voluptuous overstuffed armchairs to sit in, with little area rugs beneath them. The smell of bread is always in the air from the bakery down the street. There are no business books as a matter of policy. A black cat named William wanders in and out of the room, makes silent assessments of various customers before choosing one. He stands beside them until they reach down to pet him and then walks away, looks for another admirer. Helen says she wants to change his name to Everyman.

When she finally steps from behind the cash register and pulls on her coat, I ask Helen, "Should we bring Ruth a book?"

"I don't know. I've brought her a whole bunch, but I don't think she's been reading like she used to. She keeps falling asleep when she reads now."

"Maybe a really tacky romance novel," I say.

"Maybe she's *living* that."

"Is he going to be there again today?"

"I suppose. It seems like he's with her all the time. I talked to him the other night when I was over. Michael had stopped by, so Joel and I went in the kitchen. He said he called her again because he'd never stopped being crazy about her, and he wanted to see if the old stuff was still there, and if it was . . . Well, he said it *is* still there, and that he wants to be with her now, no matter what. It's kind of suspicious, if you ask me."

"Exactly," I said.

"I mean, maybe he just likes the drama."

"Right."

"But," Helen sighs. "I like him. I mean, I can't help it."

"I know," I say, and I do. Joel Fratto is the male equivalent to Ruth: bright, irreverent, handsome, irresistible. And best of all, not scared by cancer. Ruth said when she told him, he went through about five minutes of shock and then he asked, "What can I do? What do you want most?" and Ruth said it had been a long time since a man put his arms around her and just held her. "So he did that," she told me. "He kissed me and then he just held me. Like a bird's egg or something, really gently. And I fell asleep. And he just stayed still for a good half-hour. When I woke up, he told me to take the wig off—it was sliding off anyway. And then he raised up my shirt and took my falsies off."

"And?" I asked.

"And it was okay," she said. And then she stopped talking.

Helen climbs the steps to Ruth's apartment ahead of me, and when she opens the door, I hear her gasp. I follow quickly, alarmed, and see Joel standing in the living room, his head completely shaved. He looks like a mannequin not quite dressed.

"What did you *do?*" Helen asks.

He grins. "Do you like it?"

"Did you do this to be like her or something?" Helen asks.

"Yeah!"

Helen stands still for a moment, staring, then takes off her coat. "How is she today?" she asks, and I note with satisfaction that there is some coolness in her tone.

"She's fine. She wants me to take her to her studio."

"Are you going to?" I ask. "Can I come?"

"Sure. L.D.'s here; she's coming, too."

I go into the bedroom and see L.D. sitting on the foot of Ruth's bed eating out of a party-sized bag of ripple chips. She, too, has shaved her head. There are faint red nicks on her too-white head, and tender wrinkles, like a baby's, revealed at the top of her neck. I swallow, start to say something, but cannot.

"Well, shut your mouth, girl, or the flies will get in," she says.

"I don't believe this!" I say.

"It's not that much of a difference," she says, and holds the chip bag out to me. "Want some?"

I shake my head no. I can't keep from staring. Whereas Joel's head is perfectly round, I see that L.D.'s has some interesting lumps.

"I *had* a fucking *crew*cut, you know. It's not that different!"

"*Okay!*"

I look at Ruth for the first time, leaning back against her pillows, holding a magazine across her chest and smiling.

"Well, do you *like* this, Ruth?" I ask. "I mean, does this make you feel better or something?"

"Yeah!" She is wearing a lavender T-shirt and blue jeans and her baseball hat, and her sneakers are on and laced tightly. It is a pleasure to see her ready to go somewhere.

"Well, fine, I'll do it, then," I say.

Behind me, I hear Helen say, "Me, too."

I turn to look at her, regretting a little her hasty support, which I realize now makes my decision a little more definite than I had meant it to be. But together we go into the bathroom.

"You go first," I tell Helen. "I'll help you do the back, and then you can help me do mine."

Helen hesitates briefly, then takes a pair of scissors from the medicine chest. She opens and closes them nervously. Then she loosens a thick strand of her hair, holds the scissors up to it. "We probably need to get nearly all of it off before we use the razor." She takes in a deep breath, then stands perfectly still, staring at her-

122   self in the mirror. Then she puts the scissors down and sits beside me on the edge of the tub. "Shit. You go ahead. I don't think I can do it."

I exhale deeply. "Good."

"But I want to!"

"Well, me, too!" I say.

Helen puts the scissors back in the medicine chest and I follow her into Ruth's bedroom. "We can't do it," she says regretfully.

"That's okay," Ruth says, laughing.

"We want to but we can't," I add.

"I know," she says.

L.D. frowns, blows up the potato-chip bag and pops it. "Wimps."

"Let's shave Sarah next time we see her as a symbol for both of us," I say.

"Oh, I'll be the fucking symbol for all of you," L.D. says. "Relax."

The phone rings, and Joel answers it, then calls Ruth. She starts to get out of bed, then sits back down on the edge quickly.

"What?" I say, moving toward her.

"I'm just dizzy for a second when I get up," she says. "It's nothing."

The rest of us look at each other and then Ruth says again, "It's *nothing*. Your blood pressure gets real low when you lie around all the time. You know that, Ann. I just need to get moving."

She goes to the phone and Joel comes into the bedroom. "How is she, really?" I ask quietly.

"I was going to ask you that." He sits on her bed, leans back on his hands, and I note with some unkind-ness the familiarity with which he does this. Has he earned it? "From what I understand, it sure doesn't sound very good, but she *looks* all right."

"She looks great," L.D. says.

"Well, I don't see how long this can go on," I say. "I mean, she was told 'weeks to months.' It's been weeks already."

Ruth comes into the room and I stop talking. She looks at me, and I see that she has heard me. "I'm not going to die," she says. "I changed my mind." And then, to Joel, "You're ready, right?"

———❧———

We are once again in Ruth's studio, this time having the party she said she wanted. When we first envisioned it, I thought Ruth would be at home lying in bed, receiving visitors one by one. Knots of women would take turns consoling each other in the kitchen. All the sounds of conversation would be low and sad.

Instead she is seated before her easel, laughing loudly, drinking wine and surrounded by other people who are also laughing. It reminds me of the first time I met her, except that this time the people are all women except for Joel. He is sitting by me at a table covered with newspaper and smears of dried paint. "She's incredible," Joel says, watching her.

"I know."

"I've never met a stronger woman."

"I know."

124   "She used to be game for anything. Anything. And she'd never complain."

"She still doesn't. I went with her to the doctor a few weeks ago and heard her tell him she's been staying up a lot at night because of pain in her back. She said, 'It's kind of bad. I sort of lie there and writhe around.' And I thought, *What?* You never told me. You never said a word about it."

Joel nodded, looked down into his paper cup of wine, then up at me. "So, what do you think, Ann? Do you think she really has a chance?"

"Do you?"

He shrugged. "I went to the library and did a lot of reading about this disease."

"Yeah?"

"Of course, the books are all old by now. No book could keep up with the progress that's being made."

"What progress is that?"

"Well, you know, I mean things happen every day."

"Uh-huh."

"They do!"

"Yeah, all right."

He looks away, crumples his cup in his hand, then looks back at me. He doesn't have to tell me what he believes will happen to Ruth. "The biggest mistake I ever made was walking away from her," he said. "Major fuck-up. She was perfect for me. I think we could have . . ." He stops, swallows, looks over at her.

"She never told me a thing about you," I say.

I don't know why I've said this.

He smiles. "I never forgot her. I never did."

"Well," I say. "Who could?"

Sarah walks by us with a camera. "Smile," she says, and Joel and I put our arms around each other.

"Get ready," she says.

Together we say, "We are."

I don't see Ruth for three days. When I call, she is cheerful and unwilling to admit to any discomfort, if she's having any. Joel is always there. I ask if he doesn't have to go to work sometimes, and Ruth laughs and says, "He's an artist, remember? He's working. He paints when I sleep."

He's staying there all the time," I tell L.D. on the phone.

"I know. The fucker."

"Well . . . I guess she wants him to, right?"

"I suppose."

"I guess it's good, right?"

L.D. sighs. "It's not that. It's not that I begrudge her any happiness. It's just that I miss her. All of a sudden I don't know what's happening anymore. I'm jealous."

"Yes," I say. "That's it. Thank you."

"For what?"

"I don't know."

"Well, you're welcome."

"Okay."

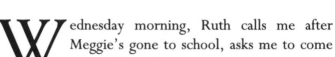

W ednesday morning, Ruth calls me after Meggie's gone to school, asks me to come over. When I get there, I see that she is alone, and I feel a sniffy kind of self-righteousness. I sit on the bed beside her, take off my coat, kiss her. "It's about time you called me."

"Ummm, your face is cold," she says. "It feels good."

"Are you hot?" I say. "Do you have a fever?"

She smiles. "No. No."

"So how are you?" I ask, and the tone is careful and ignorant.

She looks at me, tears in her eyes. "He's been here way too much, hasn't he?"

I look down, shrug.

"Do you feel like I've rejected you?"

"No, of course not!"

"Do you feel like I've rejected you?"

"Look," I say, "it's good that he showed up."

"Do you feel—"

"I don't know!" I say. "I mean, I miss you, that's all. I got used to being here."

"I told him to leave."

"Why?"

Ruth smiles, shrugs. "Oh . . . you know. What's

the point? It's too late. God. Did you ever hear of worse timing?''

"What do you mean, 'too late'?''

She looks at me as though she is trying to memorize me. I don't say anything. I'm afraid to.

"Did I ever tell you that I sort of . . . broke in on Jani and Eric?'' Ruth asks.

"No. What do you mean?''

"It was right after I found out about her. Before I went into the nuthouse. I'd been out to dinner with Michael, and then dropped him off at a friend's house to sleep over. And then I went to Eric's. I wanted to talk to him again, about . . . I wanted him to let me come home. I thought if he saw me again, he'd change his mind. I walked up to the door, and I heard this music coming from inside. Thelonious Monk. And you know, Eric hardly ever listens to music. Especially good jazz. Clearly this was a courtship thing.''

She stops talking, holds up a hand. "Wait.'' She rests for a moment, then says, "So I went up to the window to look in, and all I saw were these shoes by the sofa, his and hers, you know. Obviously, they were in the bedroom. So I went in.''

"Jesus.''

"Yeah. I went in, really quietly.''

"Oh, Ruth.''

"I started up the stairs to the bedroom and then I heard their voices, they were sort of panicked, they must have heard me. I was just going to open the door when Eric opened it. He was in his bathrobe and his glasses were off and his hair was all messed up and it just . . . I was just enraged! I bought him that bathrobe! I

128 pushed past him into the bedroom and there she was, lying there with her hair all messed up, too."

"I can't believe you did that," I said. "And I can't believe you didn't tell me when you did!"

"It gets worse," Ruth says. "I went up to her and said I'd heard so much about her and it was so nice to meet her and I put out my hand for her to shake. And I meant it to be really mean and sarcastic and everything, but all of a sudden I had this thought: *Wait. We're both women, here. Let's talk.* Of course, she didn't want to talk. She didn't want to shake hands, either. And I just stood there for the longest time, my hand reaching out to her."

She stops talking, looks at me. I say nothing.

"So she says," here Ruth adopted a whiny, nasal tone, " 'Well, I don't think this is very *respect*ful. This isn't very nice.' "

"Are you kidding?"

She holds up her right hand. "The God's truth. That is exactly what she said. Anyway, after that, Eric sort of threw me out."

"Well . . ."

"I know, I know I was wrong. But I'd thought . . . oh, I don't know, I thought he'd never *really* prefer anyone to me. In spite of all that had happened between us, I was surprised to see him that way. I'd wanted him to let me come home. I wanted to go home. But I saw pretty clearly then that it wasn't going to happen. Anyway, the next day I called him and apologized and told him to apologize to her, too."

"You did?"

"Yes. And the day after that I called you and told you I wanted to die."

"Yes, I remember that day. We were eating fried chicken. You were eating sleeping pills."

She smiles, looks around her room, then at me. "That's why I wanted Joel around. So I could have some things back. Do you understand?"

"Yes. Of course."

"I'd been feeling better. I was happy again. And I can't help it, I like men to like me."

"I know. We all do, goddamn it."

"I actually started to think I was going to make it, too. I thought if I just believed I was going to live, if I acted like it, I would. But I'm not going to make it, Ann. I know that."

"No you don't."

"I know that and you do too, and so does everyone but L.D."

I swallow, feel like crying, but I won't.

"I feel like shit, Ann. I really feel terrible."

"Why didn't you tell me? What's wrong?"

"I didn't tell you because I was feeling great. Really! But then yesterday, the same stuff started happening. I can't breathe, my back hurts so bad, especially at night. And I feel like . . . I feel so . . . sort of . . . vague, you know? It's not just weakness, it's vagueness."

"Did you take—"

"Yes, I did everything. I called the doctor, I took the pills. I think it's just my time, now."

"Well . . ." I look around the room helplessly,

130   wonder what to do. I don't know what to do. "Have
you told anyone else?"

"You do that."

"You want me to tell people?"

"Yes. Okay? I want to feel . . . free." She leans
back against the pillows, closes her eyes.

I look at the top of her head. It is rosy pink, delicate flesh. I put my hand there and feel the heat of her
life, I feel life. "Don't go," I say, a quiet, involuntary
request, and she smiles, a tiny thing, full of fatigue and
empty of hope.

"Ruth."

She opens her eyes, hands me an envelope lying
next to her. It is full of the pictures Sarah took at the
party. Looking at them, I see now that we are all too
bright, all desperate and pretending, but with our fear
betraying us anyway. The last photo is a double exposure, showing Ruth as being in two places at once. She
looks see-through, sitting squarely before her easel, but
also floating slightly above herself, looking off to the
side and reaching out toward something. She sees me
looking at it, takes it from me and looks at it again herself.

"It's a double exposure," I say. "That's all."

She smiles bitterly. "Come on. You know better
than that."

That night after dinner, I pack a suitcase. Meggie is sitting on the bed watching me. One of her sneakers is untied, and I bend down to tie it for her. Ruth helped me pick those sneakers out. I put my face in my hands, then I feel Meggie's hand on the top of my head. "It's okay," she says. And then, again, "It's okay, Mommy."

I look up at her, attempt a smile.

"When are you coming home?" she asks.

"In not too long, I think, Meggie."

"In two days?"

"I don't know, honey. Maybe. I don't know. But Daddy will be here. He's going to go to the office just while you're at school. Then he'll work from home in the afternoons, so he'll be here with you. That'll be kind of fun, huh?"

She nods.

"And I'll call you every day. And you can call me if you need to. Whenever you want."

"Okay."

I get up from the floor, sit beside her on the bed. "I'll miss you, but I really need to be with Ruth now, okay?"

Another nod. "Is she going to die now?"

"I think so."

"When will you?"

"Not for a long, long time. Not until I'm a very old lady. Not until you're an old lady yourself."

"Oh. How do you know?"

"Well," I say. "I just do."

She is visibly relieved. And in her acceptance of my false assuredness, I find relief, too. Ruth once told me, "I think one of the reasons we have children is to believe everything all over again. And I'm not talking Santa, here, either."

———— ⌒ ————

We keep everyone away that first night. Ruth says she wants to settle into herself, think about what to do. "All I know right now," she says, as we lie in her bed together that night, "is that I want to be here. I want you guys around me. You and L.D. and Sarah and Helen. And Michael, of course. He's coming home from school tomorrow night. Those are the only people I want here anymore. I don't want to have to deal with anyone else."

"What if Eric wants to come?"

"No. We've said our good-byes."

"I'll bet."

"It wasn't so bad," she says. "It was actually kind of nice. We had an hour-long phone conversation last night. We've made peace with each other."

"And what about Joel? He wants to be here, I know."

"Oh, I know, but . . ." She shrugs. "I don't want him to come. Something changes when men are around, even good ones."

I shake my head. "It's so funny that he just appeared like that. I like him. And I feel so bad that . . . I think you could have been . . .''

''It doesn't matter,'' she says. ''That just doesn't matter anymore.'' There is such private peace in her voice. I can't know how she got to where she is now. I can only see that she is there. She turns on her side, faces me. ''Listen, you need to get this, okay? I'm okay about dying. I am. I just want to do it as right as I can, I want some control. I mean, I don't want a religious service. And I want all of you to say something about me at the funeral. Will you?''

''Oh, God, Ruth.''

''And I want you to take me to a cemetery tomorrow. I think I know where I want to be buried. Sarah found it; she likes it, too. My spot would be by water. And there are two trees there that will bloom in the spring.''

I swallow, nod okay.

''That will be good, to have flowers there every spring, won't it?''

''Yes.''

''And I want an angel on my grave. A grown-up woman angel, with huge wings that look really powerful. Like she works out. I've been dreaming about angels. I think they're real. I want one on my grave.''

''Okay.''

''So that's it. Tomorrow you'll take me to the cemetery. And then tell the others they can come visit whenever they want. And we'll just . . . wait. Okay?''

''Okay.''

She sighs. ''Okay.''

''Ruth?''

"Yeah?"

"Do you really think this is it? I mean, doesn't this feel . . . impossible?"

"Not any more." She puts her hand over mine, holds it. "I'm sorry."

I start to cry and she says, "Don't. It's okay. It's okay. I feel . . . like I'm behind the camera now, and not in front of it, do you know what I mean?"

"No," I say. "I don't know what you mean. I feel terrible." I cry harder.

"Stop it," she says. "Listen to me. My perspective is different. I see everything differently. I'm telling you that it's okay and I want you to believe me. In some perverse sort of way, I'm looking forward to it. I mean, I finally get to see what happens, you know what I mean?"

I nod. "I guess so."

"The only scary thing is how alone I'll be, doing it. I mean, even with you here. I wish I could get together a bunch of women like me—God knows we're all over the place. I could round up a bunch of us terminal breast cancers and we could jump off a cliff together, like those buffalo. We could all experience death in the same way, at the same time, and then it wouldn't be lonely. We'd all die together. And then we'd all rise up together, check each other's teeth for lipstick before we entered the pearly gates."

"Wait a minute," I say. "What are you talking about? What buffalo?"

"Someone told me this, I forget who. That's how the Indians got their buffalo, they chased them over a cliff. I suppose the Indians thought they were pretty clever. But I think maybe those buffalo knew, that they chose that way to die. It was better than arrows, better than dying one by one.''

"It's like *Thelma and Louise*,'' I say. "They went off a cliff together rather than be killed the other way.''

"I know. They were the real Buffalo Gals.''

We stare at each other. There is a moment, and then we are both laughing. I get the TV guide and we watch a rerun of *The Dick Van Dyke Show*. Then Ruth is tired, wanting to go to sleep, so I make my bed in the living room. Ruth sits in a chair, supervising. "Get that flowered quilt out of the linen closet,'' she says. "You can't put that ugly plain one next to your skin.'' Then, abruptly, "I want you to make more friends.''

I look up at her, surprised.

"I'm worried about you,'' she says. "What will you do without me?''

I shrug, put the pillowcase on the pillow, throw it on the bed.

"Ann?'' she says.

"What?''

"I'm really glad you're here.''

"Me, too.''

"Come tuck me in.''

I follow her into her bedroom. Her gait is slow, slightly unsteady. She crawls under her blankets, pulls them up high. "Keep my shade open. I want to see the stars. I always like to see the stars before I go to sleep.''

"Okay.''

"Remember when we slept under the stars?''

"Yes.''

"You kissed me.''

"I know."

"Good night," she says, and I lean down and kiss her cool and perfect forehead. There is no fever here. Her forehead is fine.

———— ❧ ————

We went camping just last summer, because I'd never gone and Ruth thought that was crazy. "You have to sleep under the stars at least once in your life," she said. "There is nothing like it."

"It's uncomfortable," I said.

"It's not."

"Yes, it is," I said. "I've been in a sleeping bag. It's not comfortable. You can't get proper alignment."

"Ann," she said, "you are lying under the fucking stars. You don't think, oh, jeez, I wonder if this is hurting my posture."

"I didn't say anything about 'posture,' " I said. "I said alignment. You just can't lie right. And it's uncomfortable. There are rocks under you. And little hills and valleys, things like that. And killer wildlife all over the place just waiting for you to go to sleep."

"I'm taking you this weekend," she said.

"Sorry," I said. "Can't make it."

"Nine o'clock Saturday night, I'm picking you up," she said. "Bring your sleeping bag and your analgesics."

We laid out our bags that night, and she was right, I looked up at the sky and it was all I thought about. I felt suspended in time and in space. I believed myself uniquely privileged at the same time that I understood my connection to the millions of humans who had done this before me and would afterward.

"Isn't it wonderful?" Ruth asked, lying beside me.

"Yes."

"Does anything else matter now?"

"No."

"Do you find that comforting?"

"Yes, but scary, too," I said.

"Are you scared?"

"Well, I don't know if 'scared' is the right word. I just feel how unimportant we are."

"But that's good."

"I don't think so. I mean, I want to mean something. I want it to matter that I'm here."

"Ah, make your mark, huh?"

"Don't you?" I asked.

"I think . . . ." she said. "I believe you make your mark inside yourself. I think we're meant to use every single thing we're given. I want to act on every impulse."

"I want more. I want someone to know I was here."

"But you still have to start with yourself," she said. "You have to let yourself know you're here. Take things in. Let things happen. Everything."

I was quiet for a long time, then said, "I know I don't do that. Do I?"

"No."

"That's what makes me scared."

"I know."

"But also, I'm not like you."

"Not in all ways."

"I don't think in any, Ruth. I mean, you're my best friend. I admire you. But we're very different."

"We're more alike than you think." She rose up, leaned over me. "Do you think I'm pretty?"

"I think you're beautiful. Everybody does."

"Have you ever thought about loving me?"

"I do, I do love you, that's what I meant."

"No. I mean, physically loving me."

"No!"

"No?"

"Well, I'm sorry, Ruth, but no, I haven't."

She put her face down close to mine. I didn't move. She put her hand along the side of my face, pushed my hair back, raised her eyebrows slightly. I didn't move. The stars surrounded her, they and her face were all that I saw. And then she pulled away, lay back down on her bag, started laughing.

"What?" I asked, embarrassed and a little angry.

"You should have seen your face!" she said.

I leaped up, lay on top of her, and kissed her passionately. Then I got back into my sleeping bag.

After a stunned moment, she said, "Well, congratulations! A plus."

"How come you're always the teacher?" I asked.

"Well," she said. "I'm not. Obviously."

I closed my eyes. I went to sleep.

It was weeks later, while I was lying in the bathtub, as a matter of fact, that it came to me that I could be pleased about what happened, that it wasn't something that diminished me, but rather made me fuller, and richer. I saw that every person is a multifaceted and complex being, worthy of respectful exploration and discovery; that this longing we can't name and try to cure with relationships might only be us, wanting to know all of our own selves. I felt like I was starting to learn, and I sort of whooped a little in happiness, like a cowgirl. Meggie, who'd been walking by the bathroom door, called in, "What happened? Are you all right?" I said that nothing was the matter, that I was just fine, just an old cowgirl taking a bath.

"You're not a cowgirl!" she said, laughing.

"Why not?" I said. "It's up to me."

"*What?*" she asked.

"Nothing," I said. Which was odd, because it was everything.

The noises of Ruth's house at night are still unfamiliar to me. It takes me a long time to fall asleep. I am also thinking, how can I just go to sleep? There must be something I can do. How can I just lie here and be sleepy and comfortable and normal and

140 have nothing be wrong with me, nothing hurting in my body? I think of Joe telling me, "You have to remember that this is happening to her, okay? You have to differentiate yourself. Or you can't help her."

"What do you know about it?" I said. "You don't know anything about it!"

"I know she wants you to stay yourself," he said. "I know she wants you to be happy."

"You don't know anything," I said.

But of course he did. I'll do Ruth no good by regretting that I'm not dying, too. But I can't help it. I regret that I can't jump off with her, hold hands, take a step and fall, looking up at the sky the whole way down.

I n the morning, I push open Ruth's bedroom door, lean in to see if she's awake. There is a flock of birds in the trees outside chattering outrageously, ruffling up their feathers, cocking their heads in the too-bright way of the mechanical toy. I've been at the living-room window drinking coffee and watching them for a while, wondering as usual at the secret kind of consensus they seem to keep. Who will decide, and at what moment, that they should take off together, fly obliquely across the winter sky in their ragged but purposeful formation? Do they know where they're going?

Ruth is sitting up, looking out the window at the same tree I've been watching. I nod a greeting, give her my coffee, then stretch out beside her. There is a slat of sun lying along her face, the light illuminating the tiny

golden hairs along her ear. Below the curl of cartilage, I
can see the reddish glow of blood in her lobe. I remember holding Meggie when she was a baby and nursing
her, seeing the same thing. She held tightly onto one of
my fingers, and we rocked slowly back and forth in
front of the tiny window in her room. I used to think
that if someone about to commit a crime looked up and
saw a silhouette on the shade of a mother rocking a
baby, it would be enough to stop them. There was
sometimes a wonderful breeze, and the curtain would
billow out dramatically, then be pulled up close against
the screen, tangolike. I would watch Meggie's face,
think of all that lay ahead of her. Someday she would say
in words what it was she wanted; someday she would
walk in the door, lunchbox clanging into her leg, and I
would open it at the kitchen sink and see what she had
chosen, what she had rejected, all without me. Every
maturational milestone seemed a miracle to me, because it was Meggie who would be doing it.

Ruth is quiet, sipping coffee and staring straight
ahead, and I close my eyes, continue thinking my own
thoughts. Today we are going to a cemetery. I wonder
how Ruth's mother would feel if she were alive, watching the daughter she held in the rocker die, driving her
to graveyards as though they were apartments for rent.
It seems the most unfair and impossible of things: how
can a baby you bring into life leave it before you? What
sense is there in that? Of course, if there is one lesson
grief teaches, it is that there is no sense in some things.
Still, I know if Ruth's mother were alive, she would
handle this, draw from the reservoir of sacred strength
that women are born with. She would wear clothes

142 whose very smell comforted Ruth, she would put on an apron and make her soup and butter her toast and help her to walk to the bathroom when she needed it; and when things turned the worst, she would not leave. Women do not leave situations like this: we push up our sleeves, lean in closer, and say, "What do you need? Tell me what you need and by God I will do it." I believe that the souls of women flatten and anchor themselves in times of adversity, lay in for the stay. I've heard that when elephants are attacked they often run, not away, but toward each other. Perhaps it is because they are a matriarchal society.

I feel Ruth looking at me, and I open my eyes. She says, "You know what I was thinking? I was watching the birds and then I started looking at the branches of the tree and I was thinking how much they look like nerve cells. And then I was thinking how everything is so connected. I mean that there must be one thing, somewhere that ties everything together."

"Yes, I think so, too."

"Do you?"

"Yes."

She readjusts herself on the pillow, takes in a breath. "What I mean is that if you could just get at the real heart of one thing, you'd understand everything else. Like linguine would have something to do with linguistics, there'd be a link there."

"Yes, right."

"You've thought this, too?"

"Yes."

She stares straight ahead, blinks. "Oh. I thought I was having profound death thoughts."

W hile we are eating breakfast, Ruth asks me if I think she should have an epitaph on her tombstone.

I shrug, a bite of food in my mouth now refusing to do anything but lie there.

"I've got a few ideas," she says. "Want to hear them?"

I say nothing.

" 'Oh boy, time to read,' " she says. "What do you think of that one?"

I smile.

"Or, 'See? I *told* you!' "

"Ruth . . ."

"Well, why not? Why not have some fun? Do you think they can do italics?"

"I don't know."

Ruth picks up a piece of French toast with her fingers, drags it through some syrup, and the absurd thought comes to me that she doesn't have to watch her calories. "Know what Helen wants on her tombstone?" she asks. " 'Oops.' Isn't that great? Or, 'Up, up and away.' "

"When were you talking about tombstones with Helen?" I ask.

"When it wasn't real," she said. "Remember when it wasn't real?"

I nod. I feel sick.

"Michael's picking us up at eleven," she says, and

144 then, when I look alarmed, "It's okay. He'll be fine. He's my son. He's not chickenshit like you."

She puts her dishes in the sink, runs water on them, then turns around, arms folded across her chest. "Here's something else I was thinking. You know how you can make donations in peoples' names to the American Cancer Society instead of sending flowers to a funeral?"

"Yes. Do you want that?"

"No. I want flowers. Really, tons of them. Tell anyone who talks about giving money to cancer to buy me roses instead. The most they can afford."

The cemetery is small, off a well-traveled, two-lane highway. "Isn't this road too busy?" I ask Ruth, as we turn down the central driveway.

"What, I might get hit by a car?" Ruth asks.

"No, I just . . ."

"She means it should be quiet, Mom," Michael says. "Right? Isn't that what you mean?"

"Right."

"Quiet for what?" Ruth asks.

"For . . . contemplation," I say.

We are out of the car, walking past rows of graves, tombstones all in careful alignment with each other. Michael stops before one that has a stone dog lying permanently bereft at the base of a tombstone, his head on his paws, his mournful eyes fixed on a vision. The name of the person is on the headstone in formal capital letters, then the dates the person lived, then a simple and essential listing of roles: father, husband, son. It occurs to me that this matter-of-fact reduction is the kind of reorientation we need from time to time, that there is a value and a comfort in being here and understanding what matters most is only who you were to someone else.

There are many flowers on the graves, some plastic, most real but frozen now, bent over as though in sympathy, the petals curled up and blackened. Ruth stops before the grave of an infant, a lamb carved into the stone above the baby's name. She stoops down, traces with her fingers the dates of life. The baby lived six weeks. I had forgotten these things happen. Maybe Ruth is old.

We stop, finally, at an open area toward the back of the cemetery. It is the last row; beyond it are only trees, black and stark against the snow. There is a bushy gully and a frozen-over stream down a little hill from us, and the noises we make flush out a large bird. There is a rapid rustle of feathers, a cry of alarm, and he is gone. Ruth watches him fly away, then points to the ground. "Here," she says. "This is it." I look around, my hands in my pockets, inspecting the area, as does Michael. I don't know what we're looking for, but we're being thorough. There are two trees, just as Ruth said. "These are dogwood, they'll be beautiful in the spring. And there'll be shade here in the summer," Ruth tells Michael. He nods, avoids looking at her. "Are you all right?" she asks, and he goes to silently hold her. Between the sleeves of his coat and his gloves, I see the exposed flesh of his wrists and I look away.

Y ou've only tried Western medicine," L.D. says. "There's so much else. Why don't you go to another country? I'll go with you. China. Tahiti. They know stuff we don't. They could help you."

Ruth smiles tiredly. We are eating an early dinner in Ruth's kitchen, the three of us, and L.D. is not happy about Ruth having selected a grave site. "L.D.," Ruth says, "at some point, we have to deal with what's happening."

"You can't give up," L.D. says.

Ruth shapes a pile of macaroni and cheese into a symmetrical mound. "My parents died in a car accident," she says. "This is better. I can . . . plan. I can make provisions, say good-bye. What is wrong with us, that we are all so afraid of what we know will happen to every single one of us?"

"I'm not afraid!" L.D. says. "But this is too soon, Ruth!"

Ruth pushes her plate away, leans back in her chair. "You know, I read about these people, in Madagascar, I think, who dig up people's bones from the grave and take them out. They take them out, like on a date! That's what you can do, L.D. You can come get me, take me out somewhere."

L.D. is silent, furious. "Where would you want to go?" I ask, more in an effort to break the tension than anything. "Outdoor café? Movie? I guess not danc-ing."

"Here," Ruth says. "Here would be good. This table. This room. Right here."

She stands up. "I'm tired. I'm going to lie down."

I carry Ruth's dishes and mine to the sink, avoid looking at L.D. Ruth's parents died when she was thirty, before I met her. But I have always felt that I knew them, somehow. I have always thought I knew exactly how it was before they died. The radio in the car would have been on, low. Her mother's purse would have been beside her, with its comb and lipstick and small calendar, with its coupons for the supermarket, and photos of Ruth and Andrew. There would have been a skidding sound, some flash of terrible warning. And just before impact, Ruth's mother would have reached toward her husband, her earring that she had put on that morning in the usual ignorant way glinting in the sun. "Jack," she would have said, "wait a minute."

Ruth is right. This way is better. She has things to say to people. And some time to say them. Behind me I hear L.D. get up and put her coat on, walk out the door and slam it. I go to the window, watch her get into her car, pull away. She'll be back, I think. But she'd better hurry up.

I go to Ruth's bedroom, thinking she'll be asleep, thinking I'll pull her door closed so that the rattle of dishes doesn't wake her up. But she's not sleeping. She's lying on her side, eyes open. Two white candles burn on her dresser top. When she sees me, she smiles.

I sit in the chair by her bed. "This is hard for her. She just needed to get out of here for a while."

"I know that."

"She thinks you're giving up."

"Well, I am. But it's time to." She pushes her pillow behind her, sits up. "How come it can't be an ordinary thing? I mean, as smooth and natural as opening a drawer or something?"

"That's how people are," I say. "We resist death. Even if we don't like it here, if we find out we're dying, we like it here."

"Not everyone resists," Ruth says. "I like how the Indians say 'It's a good day to die.' We ought to be like that."

"Well, it's hard to be like that!"

She sighs, smiles. "I know. I'm mostly full of shit. I think a lot about what I'll miss. I mean, as though I *will* miss it, as though I'll be standing around somewhere wringing my hands and looking down, like in movie heavens. And you know, it's all the simplest stuff I'd miss. Sounds, you know, the clink of a teaspoon on a saucer. Folding towels. The way the moss grows up through the cracks on the sidewalk. I wonder why I was so wild and reckless when all I ever really wanted was so ordinary. I fought so hard against what I needed most. I made such big mistakes."

"Eric was not a wonderful man," I say. "I wish you'd stop feeling bad about leaving him."

"I know," she says. "I can't. Isn't it funny?"

"No," I say.

W hat I really didn't get," Helen says, "is why they were so desperate to feel us up. I mean it. I remember being at the drive-in the first time I let a guy feel my boobs. It took him about five hours to get my damn bra unhooked, and he was *pant*ing and *wheez*ing like he was an asthmatic and I was feeling nothing. I mean *noth*ing! I was looking out the window at the car next to us, and it was a family, you know, a mom and dad and two little kids in their jammies and the mom had fallen asleep, her head was against the window and her glasses were all crooked. And I just wanted to shove this guy off me and go get in the car with that family. And then he finally gets to my boob and just . . . *holds* it, like it's his fucking *lunch* money or something!"

It is Friday night, late. We are sitting on the floor in Ruth's bedroom. Ruth is in bed, and the rest of us are leaning against the wall facing her. We look like a lineup accused of some eccentric crime. "Well," Sarah says, "for him, touching you was like . . . I don't know, I mean they fantasize for what, months? years? about feeling a real breast. So when they do, that's enough. To just feel it."

"Well, it was cold," Helen says. "I remember feeling a little breeze against my nipple and thinking, God, this is so weird. I'm sitting here in a car with my boob hanging out like laundry. And then that guy came around with the flashlight, you know, the morals squad?

150   so I smacked my date on the top of his head to make him quit. He came up like a fish, I swear, his eyes all pop-out and his mouth hanging open.''

I am laughing so hard and I think, God, this is strange. This is the best time I've ever had.

L.D. has been cleaning out her fingernails with the small blade of her Swiss army knife. Now she snaps the blade closed and says with disgust, ''How could you have done that? What was the point? You weren't having any fun!''

''Well, did *you* have fun the first time?'' Sarah asks L.D.

''Absolutely. We knew exactly what we were doing.''

''How did you know?'' Helen asks.

''We were alike,'' L.D. says. ''The translation was simple.''

We are all quiet for a moment, thinking. I suppose we are all imagining L.D. making love for the first time, and for me, anyway, the thought is a tender thing.

Suddenly Ruth lifts up her nightgown, baring her chest. ''What's this?'' she asks.

No one answers, and she says, ''A back.'' And then, into the awkward silence, ''That's a joke, you guys.''

Saturday morning, Joe calls and asks if he and Meggie can come to visit. "Of course," I say.

"What should I tell Meg?" he asks, in a low voice.

"What do you mean?"

"About, you know, what to expect."

"I don't think you have to tell her anything other than you're coming to visit Ruth."

"Well . . . Don't you think she'll be scared?"

"We are talking about *Meg* here, right?"

He says nothing. I know where he is. He is standing in the kitchen, talking on the blue wall phone. The receiver has a hairline crack down one side from my once dropping it, and I have noticed that Joe and I both seek that crack out—both of us with our ring fingers, in fact—when we are talking on it. I suppose we find imperfections comforting, as people do. I imagine Joe holding the phone now, feeling the crack, looking at the floor, noticing and not noticing the crumbs under the kitchen chairs and thinking, how will I do this, do I have to do this? I've stood in that same spot.

"Just come," I say. "It's not as bad as you think."

"Should I bring something?"

"I think all we need is paper towels," I say. "But wait, I'll ask." I go into the bedroom, then come back to the phone. "And a couple of boxes of doughnuts. Not little ones. Big ones. Bow ties and cinnamon coffee

152 rolls, the big ones. And go to McDonald's and get a Sausage McMuffin.''

"L.D.'s there, huh?'' he asks.

———— ❧ ————

When L.D. came back—two hours after she left—she told Ruth she was taking her to the airport. "Just to browse,'' she said.

"I don't think I can do that,'' Ruth said. "I can't walk very far, L.D.''

"Then I'll push you in a wheelchair. They have wheelchairs there.''

"I don't know. I don't think I want to.''

L.D. looked at me, wanting an ally.

"Well, what do you mean, '*browse?*' '' I asked. "What does that mean?''

"Why don't you learn the language?'' L.D. asked. "You've been in this country a long time. Now go start my car, so it's warm for her. I don't want to talk anymore about this.''

"She doesn't *want* to, L.D. She's too tired.''

"Oh, I'll go,'' Ruth said. "What the hell. I need out. What should I wear?''

L.D. handed me her keys. "Start the car. I'll help her get dressed.''

When I came back in, Ruth was in a sweater and jeans, her high-top sneakers tied into neat bows. Her wig was on, slightly askew, and I straightened it. L.D. was in the bathroom, and I whispered, "Why are we going to the *air*port?''

"Because she said to."

"Are you afraid of her?" I asked. "Do you want to do this?"

"No," Ruth said. "And yes."

L.D. came out of the bathroom, put Ruth's coat on her. "Can you make the stairs?"

Ruth said she could, but halfway down it was clear that she couldn't. L.D. carried her the rest of the way, then helped her into the car, assigned me the rear seat. It was hard to sit there, because of the incredible pileup of junk on the floor. My knees were almost to my chin, my feet resting on empty food containers, shoes, paperbacks, random pieces of clothing, junk mail, and mysterious looking tools from L.D.'s landscaping business. I was curious about what they were, but didn't want to ask any questions. Up front they were listening to k.d. lang and L.D. wouldn't tolerate any interruptions of her. I'd made that mistake once.

Inside the main terminal, L.D. found a wheelchair and pushed Ruth up to various monitors showing departure times. "Where would you go?" she asked. "New Orleans? San Francisco?"

Ruth smiled, said nothing.

"Paris?"

She stopped smiling then, turned around in her chair. "What's up, L.D.? I mean, what do you want me to say?"

"Just . . . I'm just asking where you'd go. If you could go anywhere you wanted."

There was a long moment of silence. All around us, people were hugging each other through the bulk of their winter coats, saying good-bye, wiping away tears.

154   I hate seeing people cry when they say good-bye.
"Don't go, then!" I always want to say. "Obviously
you love each other! So don't go!" But of course they
have to, and they do. Every day. Everywhere. It's the
ones who are left behind at the gate that I worry about,
those with their hand pressed uselessly against a huge
plate-glass window, watching, while outside engines
roar so loud that no matter what you say, you can't be
heard above them.

An announcement for a flight leaving for Phoenix
made me jump, and Ruth finally said, "Well, I've never
been to Arizona. They have coyotes there. And desert.
I'll bet the moon looks bigger."

L.D. pushed Ruth to the nearest airline desk and
told the curly haired, sleepy looking agent that she
wanted two round-trip tickets to Phoenix, first class,
dates open. While the agent pushed blankly at the keys
of her computer, I felt L.D. looking at me. I didn't
move. I stared straight ahead. Some people pray, I was
thinking. Others buy airplane tickets.

———— ❧ ————

Meggie brings Ruth two presents: a book of
riddles, and a Baby Ruth. She puts them
down on the kitchen table, then points to the
candy. "Get it?" she asks. "A Baby *Ruth*."

"You," Ruth says, pulling Meggie to her, "are a
very clever girl. Are you in college yet?"

"No. Only fourth grade."

"Unbelievable."

"Is that your wig?" Meg asked.

"Yes."

"Oh."

A little moment, and then Ruth asks gently, "Would you like to see how my real hair looks?"

Meg nods. Ruth pulls her wig off, bends her head down low so Meggie can see the top of her head. Meg stares wide-eyed and I see her fingers curl into the safety of her hand. "Does it hurt?" she asks.

"Well," Ruth says. "Not like when you cut yourself. More like when you miss someone."

"Oh." A big breath in. "Remember when you built the snow lady with me?"

There have been times in the past when I have been proud of Meggie. And there will be many times more to come, I know. But none will surpass this moment. She's only nine. It would be all right for her to pull away, out of fear, out of strangeness. But she doesn't. She looks up fully into Ruth's face and she is smiling. Love is there.

"I certainly do remember that snow lady," Ruth says. "You couldn't say 'lady' then. You said 'yady.' "

"Yes," Meggie says. "I remember. I was little. I was only three."

I remember too. It was shortly after I'd met Ruth. She baby-sat for me while I went to get groceries. I'd been having a bad week. The prospect of standing before the tomato bin for as long as I wanted with no one yanking at my sleeve seemed roughly equivalent to a week at Canyon Ranch spa. And I did stand before the tomatoes for a good long time. I also looked at every single kind of cereal. I pressed the buzzer for the butcher, just because I had time to wait for a special cut. I got rack of lamb, which I knew nothing about, including how to cook it. I just wanted it. I was hoping the check-out clerk would say admiringly, ''Oh, rack of *lamb*,'' and I would say, ''Yes.''

When I came home, I'd found a snow woman, wide-hipped and big-breasted, standing beside the lamppost in my front yard. She wore a wreath of evergreen around her head, and her arms were shaped so that it looked as if her hands were on her hips. She had an attitude, even as she melted.

I see Joe signaling to me out of the corner of my eye, and I follow him into Ruth's bedroom.

''What?'' I ask.

''How are you?'' he says quietly.

''I'm okay. It's okay. You know.''

He nods, then says, ''Now, don't misinterpret this, okay?''

''What?''

''I want you to stay as long as you need to.''

''*What,* Joe?''

''I just wondered, you know, do you have any idea how long this might take?''

A small rush of air comes out of me as though I've been punched. ''Go home, okay?'' I say. ''I don't know. I don't know how long. I don't fucking think about it. I'm just here. For Christ's sake.''

Joe sags into himself, takes my arm. ''You're

doing just what I asked you not to. You're misinterpreting this. I only mean . . .''

I wait, say nothing.

"I guess I mean how do you think she's doing?"

"Is that what you mean, Joe?"

"Yes!"

Behind us, we hear Meggie calling. She comes into the bedroom, holds up half of the candy bar. "We shared this. Can I have mine now?"

"Yes," I say. "You sit here and eat it, and let's let Daddy talk to Ruth."

Joe goes into the kitchen, and I sit with Meggie on Ruth's bed. "Don't get chocolate on her sheets," I say. "These are very fancy sheets. They come from France, and Ruth likes to keep them nice."

"They come from France?" Meggie asks.

"Yes."

"Why?"

"I don't know," I say. "I guess they have good cotton there."

"Can I lie on them?"

I nod, hold out my hand for her candy bar, and she puts her head down on the sheet. She holds extremely still, her eyes wide and unblinking. She is a member of the Junior Scientists of America Club, carries her signed-in-cursive membership card in her red plastic wallet. Finally, disappointed, she sighs and sits up. "They just feel like mine."

"Really?" I lie down myself. The truth is, I don't feel any difference either and I tell Meggie this.

"Maybe Ruth is like that pea princess, and she can feel better than us."

"I think that must be it."

"Ruth gave me a teapot," Meggie says. "The blue one on her counter."

"Did she?"

"Yes, there's a dragonfly on it."

"I know. It's very pretty."

"I will keep it forever," Meggie says.

"I don't blame you."

When Joe comes to get Meggie, his eyes are red. He hugs me good-bye, says into my ear a quiet "I'm sorry."

"Yes," I say. "I'll call you later."

He and Meggie are going to Bradlee's to get light bulbs. I am ashamed at what I am feeling: I want to go, too. I want to walk up and down long aisles, saying, "Let's see. Q-tips? Do we need shampoo?" I want doormats and polyester blouses and matched sets of mixing bowls to be the only thing in my head. I want to look at stupid Barbie dolls with Meg, buy her a new one with hair down to its knees and breasts forever high and full.

That night I dream that I invite many dying people for dinner. The table is long and rectangular, covered with a white tablecloth. One man, his fingers eaten nearly away by some terrible disease, looks down at his hands, smiling sadly and saying he was a pianist. Then he looks up and says, "I used to love my hands so much." There is a couple there, both of them very old, and they want to sit together but people keep saying, no, you should mix with the others, you always sit together. One woman whose husband died ten years ago says she visited his grave every day for three years. Then she decided it was enough, and she simply stopped going. I have a vision of the man's grave as she is describing it. The number of years he's been buried is written on it and the numbers change, click up like those in a gas pump. It says 17, then 25, then 50, until finally it's 200 and you realize everyone who knew him is dead, too. It is profoundly comforting. The phone rings and I jerk awake and grab it quickly. "Yes?" I whisper into the receiver. It's Joe, saying, "You're not sleeping, are you?"

"Yes."

"It's only eight-thirty!"

"She was really tired tonight. She went to bed at seven. I read for a while and then I figured I'd just go to sleep, too. I'll get up early. It's actually nice to get up early."

Silence, and then, "So how's it going?"

"It's all right."

"It was so weird to see her, knowing I probably won't see her again."

"Yes."

"Know what she said?"

"What?"

"That the hardest thing is she doesn't know when it's coming. She'll feel a little dizzy, and think, is this it? She said she was on the toilet and she felt that way, and she didn't know whether she should get out and arrange herself or not."

Here is the ache back, the lazy and insolent spreading out in the center of my chest of the diffuse heaviness I hadn't realized I'd been without. "I know. We don't know what to expect."

"She said mostly it felt like falling really slowly, in a place that had no light. And no sound."

"She did?"

"Yes."

"God."

"But you know what? I don't think she's scared."

I say nothing. I am thinking, *Why doesn't she tell me things like that? Why must she keep holding something between us? I am here to be here.*

"Is Meggie all right?" I ask.

"She's fine. Laura's spending the night. At the moment they're eating cucumber sandwiches. They read about it somewhere."

"She'll be crabby tomorrow. Whenever Laura sleeps over, they never go to sleep. They wake each other up all night, go downstairs and turn on the television, looking for sex."

"How do you know that?"

"She told me once, when she was in a good mood." I hear a noise coming from Ruth's bedroom, and whisper hastily, "I have to go. She's up. I'll call you in the morning."

I go into Ruth's room, see her sitting at the edge of the bed. "What time is it?" she asks.

"Eight-thirty."

"It's so dark out!"

"Well, yes, it's eight-thirty."

"At *night?*"

"Yes."

"Oh. I thought it was morning."

"No. You've only been asleep for an hour and a half."

"I think I'm hungry."

I turn on her overhead light. "Then let's go eat."

She turns out the overhead, turns on her bedside lamp. "I hate overhead lights. They're gross."

"Sorry."

"It's okay."

She reaches for her flannel shirt, pulls it on, starts to stand up, and falls back down. I reach out toward her and she waves me away. "I can do it."

She takes in a breath, waits, then rises slowly. "See?"

We go into the kitchen, and she puts a slice of bread in the toaster. "I was thinking cinnamon toast," she says.

"Okay."

"Do you want some?"

"No."

She sits in the chair, looks over at me with weary tenderness. "Thank you for staying with me all the time."

"You're welcome. I'll bill your estate."

"No, really. It's really nice of Joe, too."

"It's no big deal. He's pretty well set up to work at home."

"It is a big deal. You tell him I said thank you, okay? You let him know that I was very grateful for what he did for both of us."

162   I nod, and find suddenly that I am starting to cry. I
put my hand over my face. "I'm sorry," I say.

"What are you sorry about?"

"I don't know. I don't want you to feel bad."

"Seeing you cry doesn't make me feel bad. It
never has."

"Right. Okay." I take my hand away, look down,
shudder slightly, then look back up again. We hold
something between us, no words, and then I say, "I
wish you'd do something for me."

"What?"

"I wish you'd forgive me."

"For what?"

"For everything wrong I ever did to you."

She smiles.

"I mean it!"

"You didn't do anything wrong to me."

"Yes, I did. I did so many wrong things I don't
have time to fix."

"No, you didn't."

"Yes, I did!"

"Okay, fine. I forgive you. Okay?"

"Do you?"

"Yes. Now get me the cinnamon down. I can't
reach that high. One thing I have always been is too
short. It's adorable when you're in junior high. After
that, it's a pain in the ass for the rest of your life."

When she recovered from her first round of chemo and radiation therapy, Ruth decided to take up swimming. I went with her, met her at the Y every Thursday evening. Once, as we sat at the side of the pool, I sighed loudly.

"What?" she said.

"I don't know. You're so little and delicate. I always feel like a jerk next to you. Like you're Princess Grace and I'm Larry Bird."

"What are you talking about?" she said. "Look at your beautiful long legs. Everybody wants that."

"I'd rather be little and delicate."

"You're one of those people who wants everything but what they have."

"The whole world's like that," I said.

"No it isn't. It's just that we are."

"Well, there you are," I said. "Close enough."

She smiled, then dragged her foot slowly up out of the water. "You'll never get divorced, Ann. Your situation is very different."

"What do you mean? I'm not even talking about that!"

She looked at me. "No?"

"No!"

"Sure you are," she said. "You always are. Ever since I got divorced, you've been wanting to be little and delicate. So to speak."

"You know, you are just not always right, Ruth."

"Oh, I know," she said. "Not always."

On the afternoons that Michael comes to visit, I leave for a while, let them have themselves to each other. Michael is impenetrably cheerful around me; I hope with her he can cry. Sometimes I go for walks outside, taking in the stubborn shape of frozen things, enjoying the give of snow beneath my boots, listening to the clear winter sounds: birds, barking dogs, children exuberantly name-calling as they disengorge from dirty yellow school buses. Other times I drive, usually aimlessly—there's no time to go home. I bring Ruth back little presents: magazines, bubble gum, quarts of soft-serve ice cream, the hand games you play with ball bearings.

Once, as I drove down a road I'd not been on before, I saw a sign in the picture window of a turquoise blue ranch house saying, PSYCHIC—OPEN. There was a clumsily drawn crystal ball with disembodied hands sporting long red fingernails hovering over it as illustration.

I pulled into the small parking lot in front of the house. There were no other cars there, and I wondered if the place was really open. I knocked on the door, and an older woman in a print housedress and a white cardigan sweater answered. She wore open-backed blue plastic slippers, and her gray hair hung long down her back. "Do you do readings?" I asked.

"Yes, of course," she said and stepped aside, waving me in. I heard children arguing behind a beaded curtain in another room, and the obnoxious droning of an exercise instructor on TV.

"Sit," she said, indicating a folding chair on one side of a card table. The room had no other furniture with the exception of religious pictures on the wall: Jesus, staring forlornly upward; Mary with a soft smile and a halo like a gold plate behind her head; the apostles sitting at their famous table. There was a rug on the floor that looked like the kind you win at state fairs, a red-and-black silken weave featuring crouching panthers.

The woman sat in the chair on her side of the table. "Now," she said. "For five dollars I can read your palm. But what *you* really need is the Tarot cards."

"Is that right?" I asked.

She nodded, lit up a cigarette from a mint-green pack, exhaled courteously up into the air.

"How much does that cost?"

She frowned deeply, her mouth like an upside-down smile. "Okay. For you, I make it cheap. Fifteen dollars. Usually it's twenty-five."

I nodded agreement, and she shuffled a well-worn Tarot deck, then put it down before me and told me to cut it. I did and she made an arrangement of cards, faced the drawings toward me. She tapped a long fingernail against a card showing a man in armor seated on a horse. Then she drew in on her cigarette, exhaled. "This is your husband," she said. "He don't get along with the ladies so well. He is of the practical nature."

I smiled.

"Sometimes you want to leave him, but . . ." She shrugged. "You don't." She looked up at me. "You are right to stay. Divorce is no good for children, you understand me? And anyway, you love this man. You got a red-haired girl, right?"

I stopped smiling.

"She is a lot like you."

"I think so."

"Yes," she said, agreeing with herself. "That is true." She turned another card over, and her forehead wrinkled. "Someone is sick," she said. "Who?"

"I . . . my friend. I have a friend who is sick."

"I don't see no cure," the woman said, turning over two more cards. She looked up again. "You must pray for your friend to accept this."

I said nothing. But then, when the silence became uncomfortable, I said, "Well, I'm . . . I don't pray, really."

She raised her eyebrows. "No?"

"No," I said. "I don't exactly believe in God. I mean, I believe in something, but not a Being who's interested in me. Aware of me. I believe . . . I think what I believe in is a Great Spirit."

The woman leaned back in her chair. She was a mix of incredulity and weariness. "Don't you know," she asks, "that God *is* a spirit?"

"Well . . . yes," I said. "Right."

"So you will pray for your friend?"

"Yes."

Let her think she has made an easy convert, I thought. This is too hard to explain.

On the way back to Ruth's, I passed a small Catholic church. I went in and lit a candle, put my head down on my arms at the kneeler, opened with, "Dear God." You try, sometimes, in spite of yourself.

I'd meant to tell Ruth what happened. I thought she'd enjoy the story, with certain omissions. But I never did.

———— ❧ ————

"After I die, you guys have really got to go on a diet," Ruth says. We are eating dinner: angel hair with a sauce Helen made that called for two sticks of butter; crusty rolls, Caesar salad. Brownies and ice cream are for dessert.

"You're supposed to gain weight in your forties," Helen says. "It's actually sexy."

"Oh, bullshit." Sarah can afford to say that. She's the only one of us who hasn't gained a lot. She sits now with her irritatingly small portions before her, with her stomach flat under her napkin. She probably belts her nightgown.

"You'd look a far sight better if you gained a few," L.D. tells her. "Way it is now, you look like an asshole. All women as skinny as you look like assholes."

Sarah looks up at her, considers saying something in response, but then changes her mind. She winds pasta around her fork, lifts a tidy bundle up to her mouth.

"You're like one of those insects, look like a stick, what are they called, walkingsticks?"

A thin silence.

"Yo, Sarah," L.D. says, "isn't that what they're called? Come on, you know everything, right?"

Ruth puts her napkin over her plate. She hasn't eaten a bite. "L.D.," she says.

"I can take care of myself," Sarah says. Then, to L.D., "What's your problem, anyway?"

L.D. points to herself in mock surprise. "I have a problem?"

"Let's have the brownies," I say, but it is as useless as though I'd said nothing.

L.D. says, "I'll tell you the problem, Sarah. I'm sick of your grim predictions. I'm sick of your CEOing Ruth's life. I think we need a new boss here. Someone who believes in Ruth's strength to goddamn overcome this. Because she has it. She has it. If people will just stop taking it away from her, she has it. I think we should plan on her getting better, not burying her!"

"It sounds to me," Sarah says, "as if you're the one trying to run things, L.D. I only did what Ruth asked me to."

"You made her ask you!"

"Please," Ruth says.

Helen stands up, grabs the pan of brownies off the counter, slams them down in front of L.D., hands her a knife. "Here," she says. "Cut these. Make them all even so we won't fight."

L.D. hesitates, then takes the knife, cuts down the center of the pan and looks up. "Who knows higher math?" she asks. "Where do I cut to make them all come out even?"

"The last time I ate really a lot of brownies, I'd taken LSD," Helen says. "It was in the Rocky Mountains, in Colorado, in 1969. I thought the brownies were alive, but I ate them anyway."

"I loved acid," Sarah says. "I could speak different languages on it. I don't mean Italian, I mean dog. I mean wind."

We are all of us stunned, and we stare at her.

"You never took acid," L.D. says, finally.

Sarah smiles, a lovely thing, brushes an invisible crumb off her lap. "It was on the back of a stamp. The first time I took it, I spent all my time looking into the center of a flower. I kept saying over and over, 'It's all right *here.*' "

L.D. grunts. "You were one of those hippies in dresses that cost three hundred dollars."

"Skirts," Sarah says. "And gauzy tops, with tassels and all those shiny things on them—sequins, rhinestones."

"Fine, three-hundred-dollar skirts and tops," L.D. says.

"Is it that you're *attracted* to me?" Sarah asks suddenly. "Is that it?"

L.D. lets air out of one side of her face. "Sorry."

"What's your girlfriend like?" Sarah asks.

"She's real little and blond and pretty," Helen says.

"And sexy," Ruth adds.

Sarah nods thoughtfully. "L.D., do you think if you're a woman you have to be a lesbian to be truly political?"

L.D. looks up sharply.

"I mean it," Sarah says. "This is a real question. I've thought that. I've often thought that."

L.D. pushes back from the table and crosses her legs man-style, booted ankle up on one knee. "Door's open," she says. "Come on in."

"I'm being serious," Sarah says.

Silence.

"If there's a heaven," Ruth says, "do you think you have to come there as you died? I mean, all beat up and stuff?"

That night, when we are alone, Ruth asks me to make oatmeal. "Don't use water, use milk. And put in a whole lot of brown sugar and butter. And some raisins."

When I carry the bowl into her bedroom, she sighs. "Put it on a tray, with one of those cut-lace placemats. Put the spoon on a napkin. There's a bud vase in the cupboard."

I carry the bowl out to the kitchen, prepare the tray in the way she asked me to, add a small glass of orange juice. I feel as though my hurt feelings are standing behind me, tapping me hard on the shoulder. When I set the tray beside her, I say, "You're so picky. You're kind of a bitch."

"I know. I always was. I'm spoiled." She inspects the tray, then looks up at me. "Go ahead and eat it."

"This is for you!"

"I know. But I can't . . . I think I'm hungry, but then I just can't eat. You eat it. Just let me watch, do you mind?"

I pick up the tray, look at it. I realize that I would never prepare such a thing for myself, but that I should. It's a good thing to occasionally lie back and wiggle your toes at the pleasure you've created for yourself. "You really want me to eat this?" I ask Ruth.

"Is it too weird? Is it sexual or something? *Is* it weird?"

Actually, I'm not sure. But I say, "No, it's okay. But don't start criticizing my manners or anything like that."

"I won't."

"No . . . you know, smiles, or anything."

"I won't!"

I eat the oatmeal and when I'm finished, she asks, "Isn't it good?"

I show her the empty bowl, scraped clean.

"On cold mornings in Montana," Ruth says, "my mother always made me that. And she'd wrap a scarf all around my head till only my eyes stuck out. I had red boots, with fur on the top. I walked to school, and it hurt, when I got there, getting defrosted. I'd gotten used to the cold."

"I remember that, too," I said. "Your fingers would feel fat around the pencil."

"Yes." She sighs, closes her eyes. "I suppose it's gross to say so, but I actually had a very happy childhood."

"Did you?"

"Yes. So this cancer, it didn't come from that."

172   "Oh, who knows where it comes from? It just comes."

"I really hope so," she says. "I'm so tired of digging around in my head, trying to figure out all I did wrong."

———— ᘒ ————

I have trouble going to sleep that night. I can feel the mild ache of fatigue in my body, but my mind is overly alert, as though it is waiting for evil to creep up on it. I change positions, turn the pillow over, then over again. And then I close my eyes and ask my brain to show me something that will make me feel comfortable and safe. I envision a gigantic nest, lodged into the high branches of a tree. Light filters in gently through the leaves; the sun is setting; a veiled moon waits off to one side of the sky. There is a thick white quilt in the nest, and a pillow. I climb in, put my head on the pillow, wrap the quilt around me. It smells like air and sunshine. I am high up and comfortable, but I need something else to feel safe. I look up at the edge of the nest and sitting there, looking down at me, are Joe and Meggie. I can't make out their features, but I know who it is from the outline of their bodies. Meggie is swinging her legs, and I see the shoelace from one of her sneakers hanging down and following the loopy pattern of her movements. The light is a rich golden color; it seems to push as strongly as a hand at their backs but they stay steady, they stay sitting there and watching over me; suddenly, thick bands of light from the last of the day's sun spread like peacock feathers all around them. They could be the center of the universe. I open my eyes, say I understand, and then close them again to sleep.

The next morning, Ruth asks me to draw her a bath. Then, after I help her in, she points to the floor. "Sit there, will you?"

She holds her washrag up, lets water run from it, watches it. "Sometimes water sort of twists," she says. "Did you ever notice that?"

"Yes."

"Why does it do that?"

"I don't know."

"There are rules about all those things."

"I suppose. I don't want to know them, though. I'd rather believe in magic."

"Me, too. That's one thing I always liked about you Ann, you don't know a lot of things. Especially about current events. You're really a moron about that stuff. And I never knew who the goddamn secretary of anything was, so it was a comfort to be around you."

"Thank you very much."

She raises a leg, looks at it critically. "It feels like I need a shave."

"I'll do it for you."

"Will you?"

"Of course."

"Have you ever shaved anyone before?"

"Sure. I've prepped people for surgery. I've

174 shaved lots of things. The men get real nervous when you get near their peckers. But I'm good. Lean back. Relax.''

I soap one leg, then slowly pull the razor up along it. Ruth laughs a little. "Does it tickle?" I ask.

"Yes. But I was also thinking how stupid this is. Who started it, anyway?"

"I don't know."

"It's such a strong thing, though," she says. "I mean, I'm lying around dying and I feel hair on my legs and I need to shave them. And I'm not even . . . involved."

"I could call Joel. You could lie on your bed with your legs hanging out and he could come admire them."

She closes her eyes. "Yes. That would be quite nice."

We are quiet then, listening to the scraping sound of the razor, the lapping of the water, the occasional drip out of the faucet. In the apartment next door, we hear a door slam loudly. "Nancy's going to work." Ruth sighs. "Every morning, she slams that door like that, as if she's really pissed off."

"Is she?"

"I don't know. I never did talk to her very much. The first time I met her, I saw that she used lip pencil."

"Ah. No wonder."

"No, I mean, it was way outside her natural lip line, you know, she'd drawn in what she wanted. Dial-a-Mouth. I didn't feel I could relate to her. Her lips looked like those cartoon animals that wear lipstick, the hippos with the pleated skirts. She was . . . yeah, she was like a cartoon woman.''

"Did she draw in eyebrows, too?''

"No,'' Ruth says, "but you could tell that was coming. She'll be the kind to draw those big fat greasy kind of eyebrows, the ones shaped like fried shrimp. I don't know, we just never had much to say to each other.''

"Well, I guess not. A woman with incipient shrimp eyebrows!''

Ruth stops smiling, and her face turns earnest. She pulls her leg away, sits up. "Do you think I've been awfully small in my life, always sort of hypercritical?''

I don't answer for a while, and she says, "You do, don't you?''

"Well, some,'' I say. "But mostly I think you just tell the truth more than most people, that's all.''

"Well, that's not bad.''

"No.''

"I have to tell you something,'' she says, and I feel myself brace for anything. But all she says is, "I'm in a good mood.''

I let the soap slide into the water, rinse my hand in a slow circle. "Yeah?''

"Well, isn't that sort of crazy? I mean, I woke up today, and I felt really, really happy.''

"Well, that's good. That's good.'' I don't understand it, but surely it must be good.

"And I have to tell you something else, Ann.''

"What?''

She draws in a breath, takes one of my hands in

both of hers. "I want to be buried here, but I want to go to Andrew's to die."

I pull her hand away, sit back on my heels. "What for? What do you mean?"

"Now, don't get crazy."

"Is this because we had that weird fight in the kitchen last night?" I ask. "That's why, isn't it? That was just some tension, Ruth. I mean, these are extraordinary circumstances. There's going to be some tension. Or do you think this is too much to ask us? It's not. We're fine here. I'm fine here. I'll stay with you."

"No. It's just . . . because he's my brother. He was there when I was born, Ann."

I say nothing. I feel a tightening in my chest that is a terrible fear.

"Can't you understand this at all?"

I nod, then shake my head. "No!"

"Well, you will. Michael can fly down there with me. Can you take us to the airport?"

"When?"

"I think we'd better plan on a few days from now."

You can't go, I want to say. We just made a whole lot of the Jell-O you like. We haven't watched the movies we rented. And beyond that: You are ours. You belong with us.

I don't say anything. I shave her other leg. I help her put on perfumed talc. She sits in a chair in an apricot-colored nightie and I change her sheets. And then we make some phone calls.

That afternoon, while Ruth naps, I stand at the window and review things that might have made her come to this decision. Did she feel my vision last night, understand how much I need my family, and start to feel guilty again about taking me away from them? Or maybe it was the time Helen and I thought she was sleeping, and talked about our fears for her. I'd said I hoped that the end wasn't respiratory, that I didn't want her to feel she was suffocating. Helen said but that was better than her brain going, wasn't it? And then we said nothing. I think we felt ashamed of ourselves. Was she awake then? I remember Helen finally saying, "I just feel like I'm dodging malignancies. All around me . . . you know? Like, if I open the window, one will slip in and get me. I just keep wondering when it will be my turn."

I hear a knock at the door. It's L.D., loaded down with daisies. "She likes these," she says, and starts for the kitchen.

I follow her, and as I watch her fill a large pitcher with water I tell her Ruth wants to go to Andrew's.

She looks sharply at me. "For a visit."

"No, L.D."

She looks away, finishes filling the pitcher with water, shoves the flowers in it, then slams them on the kitchen table. She sits down, staring at them, then looks up at me. "Will you stop your fucking sighing? You're

178 driving me crazy! I never heard anyone sigh so much in my life!''

I open my mouth, then stop. I had no idea. ''Well, I'm sorry. I didn't realize—''

''You sigh when you're making dinner. You sigh when you're looking at magazines. You sigh when you're just fucking sitting there doing nothing!''

I take a small step forward, then another, then lean down to put my arms around her. ''We didn't do anything wrong,'' I say. ''She just wants to go to her brother's house. It's not our fault.''

Her arms come up out of her lap and she holds on to me fiercely. ''It is. It's my fault. I won't let her die. And she knows it. So she's going somewhere where she can.''

''I don't think that's it, L.D.''

''Where is she?''

''Taking a nap.''

She nods. ''I'll wait.''

Of course Helen and Sarah claim responsibility as well. We all of us feel like the one who stood up in the boat at the wrong time. The four of us are talking about it in low voices while we eat dinner that night. We made fried chicken, mashed potatoes, buttered green beans and corn, apple pie. This is what we do. We accept, like a backrub, the relief of calories. Helen is saying that maybe Ruth feels bad that she's taking so long to die, like women and orgasms, she's saying. Suddenly, Sarah holds up a hand, stops chewing. I hear it now, too, Ruth, moaning. We move together into her room. Her light is on, and she is sitting at the side of her bed. She looks up, her face full of pain. "My back," she says.

I rummage through the pills at the side of her bed. "I did," she says. "It didn't help."

I stand still, thinking, I am a nurse. I should know what to do. What should I do? Nothing comes to me except a knocking sense of panic. For the first time, I think this is just too much for me, she needs to be in the hospital.

Then L.D. pushes through us, picks Ruth up and carries her to the rocking chair in the corner of the bedroom. "Give me a blanket," she says, and I hand her the quilt from the bed. She tucks it tightly around Ruth, then rocks her slowly, staring intently into her face. "Think of whiteness," she says. "Think of stillness." Then, her voice lowering and softening and slowing, "Think of how the dust rises up from the horses' hooves. Do you know how the cactus flowers? Think of that, Ruth, think of it opening, slowly, so slowly." Ruth moans, a sound like "Ahhh." If you didn't know, you'd think it was something altogether different.

This is what I keep thinking, sitting in the living room with Helen and Sarah. Pretend this is something else. I am waiting for Ruth to finish getting her hair permed. Then we will go and look at shoes: dangerous high heels. Jeweled sandals that we will try with our socks on because both of us hate our toes. Sarah sits motionless, her hands folded on her lap. Helen holds the dishcloth, folds it and unfolds it, folds it again. We look at each other from time to time. We can hear L.D., the low murmur of her comfort over Ruth's moans, and then finally it is only L.D. we hear.

"Did she die?" Helen asks. "Oh, Jesus, did she die?"

The air around me holds me down. I swallow against the strength of something that is telling me not to move anything, not even to breathe.

Then we hear L.D. close Ruth's door, and come into the living room. "She's sleeping."

She sits down beside Sarah, puts her arm around her, and for the first time I see Sarah weep. "I don't know what's so surprising about this," she says. "I don't know what I thought was going to happen."

The day before she is to leave, Ruth sits at her kitchen table trying to eat breakfast. She is feeling better, but taking her morphine pills regularly to head off what might happen again. This makes her pleasantly spacey, blurred at the edges. She is putting a few Cheerios at a time into a bowl of milk, then spooning them up and eating them. "This way they stay crisp," she says. "You should really try it, Ann." Someone left a newspaper from yesterday on the table and she pulls it over to her, starts leafing through it. I know what she's looking for: both of us always read our horoscopes, take them seriously. She comes to the obituaries and stops, gasps.

"What?" I say.

She points to a name. I can't quite see it upside down, so I come around to her side of the table, look down over her shoulder. "Ruth Thomas," it says.

"What is this?" I say, furious, pulling the paper away from her. "Who did this?"

"It's not me," Ruth says.

"What do you mean?"

"It's not me! It's another woman with the same name." She pulls the paper back, spreads it on the table, and together we read about the other Ruth Thomas. She was out on a hike, climbing up a mountain. She fell. She was thirty-eight, a stockbroker.

"Jesus," Ruth says.

I sit down, say nothing. I am thinking, for some reason, of the suits in the other Ruth's closet, hanging there.

"Isn't that weird?" Ruth asks.

"It really is."

"Do you think it's a sign or something?"

"Oh, Ruth. Of what?"

She looks at me. "You're tired."

"Yes, I suppose."

"You don't want me to go."

"No."

"I just don't think I can explain it anymore."

"It's okay. I want you to do what you need to."

She nods. "Want to help me pack?"

We are deciding what underwear she should bring when we hear the door open. "Probably Sarah," Ruth says. "She said she'd stop by before work."

It is not Sarah, though. It is Joel, holding a bakery bag and a white, long-stemmed rose. "I know what you told me," he says. "But I wondered . . ." He looks at the open suitcase on Ruth's bed, then at her.

"I'm going to my brother's," she says. "In Florida."

He nods, then asks, "Why?"

"I just need to. Full circle, something like that. I'm not sure I can explain it. But things are not . . . I'm not going to get better, Joel."

He stands still, then puts the bag and the flower down. "Want some help?"

"I don't think so."

"I just wanted to see you again, Ruth."

"That's okay."

He crosses over to her, puts his arms around her, and I leave the room, close the door behind me.

In a few minutes, he comes out, eyes reddened, and goes to the door. "I don't know why I came back. She asked me not to."

"I'm sure she didn't mind."

"Do you think there's *any* chance she might come back here?"

I look slowly around at her living room, then at Joel.

"Okay," he says, and, with exquisite care, closes the door behind him.

I t is late at night. Ruth and I are lying in her bed, arms around each other. I am crying quietly, blowing my nose into Kleenex after Kleenex.

"You should take my plants," she says. "And I want you to have all my rocks and seashells. And the birds' nests. I'm giving my books to Helen."

"I don't want to take anything," I say. "I want to leave things for you to come back to."

She nods, and I see the shine of tears in her eyes as she looks around her bedroom. "I don't think I'm coming back, though."

"But I *want* you to," I say. I am being nonsensical. I am acting like a child, I know it. This can't be helping her.

"I will come back as a little breeze," she says. "You will feel me on your face, and you will know that I'm still listening. So you can still talk to me."

"Okay."

"I want you to always talk to me. I think I'll hear."

"Yes, all right."

"You guys help Michael clean out this place when I die. I don't want him to have to do it alone. Eric said he'd help, but I don't want him to. I don't want him touching my stuff, even if I have forgiven him. And I want you to come over real early on that day, throw away anything that might be embarrassing." Her eyes widen suddenly and she says, "Take my vibrator, okay?

184 You have to take that with you tomorrow! I don't want anyone to find that.''

"I'll build a glass case for it," I say. "Give it a plaque. TEN ZILLION HOURS OF USE, AND STILL WORKING.''

She closes her eyes. "Are you sleepy?" I ask. "Don't go to sleep.''

She opens them again. "All right. But stop crying.''

"I am.''

"No, you're *not.*''

"How do you know? Maybe this is allergies.''

"You're so full of shit.''

"I love you, Ruth.''

She rubs my arm, sighs.

The phone rings, and she says, "Let the machine get it. I've said good-bye to everyone. I don't want to say it anymore.''

We hear Helen's little-girl voice saying, "Ruth, are you awake? I just wanted to call you again. I just wanted to talk to you. Ann?" A long pause, and then she hangs up.

"Was that mean?" Ruth asks.

"I don't think so. I think she'll understand.''

"You all should stay close, take care of each other," Ruth says. "Each of you has so much. Have you seen that?''

"Yes.''

"I want you to stay in touch with every single one of them," she says. "You especially. You need them.''

I am thinking that I know I won't. That everyone might try, but that, inevitably, I will pull into myself, keep my distance. I am going to lose Ruth, and she is not replaceable, and that is all. But I say, "Yes, I'll keep in touch with everyone. L.D. and I have plans to go bowling next Thursday." Actually, this is true.

Ruth nods, turns to look out the window. "Open the curtains some more, will you? I think Venus is really close to the moon. I love when that happens."

I open the curtains wide, sit on the floor beside her bed. There's not a cloud anywhere; it's a good show tonight.

"I hope Andrew puts my bed by the window," she says.

"I'll call him tomorrow when you're flying out there. I'll tell him to. And I'll tell him to get wild strawberry Jell-O and good sheets. Some purple freesia, to keep next to you."

"Yes, okay."

I look out the window for a while, thinking of what else I'll need to tell Andrew. "Let her do whatever she wants," I'll say. "She may all of a sudden ask to go to the movies. You should take her." There is a bright star, close to one end of the crescent moon and slightly below it, as though it is hanging by a string. "Is that Venus?" I ask. Nothing. "Ruth?"

I turn around, look at her. She is sleeping, a weariness in her face so profound that it literally takes my breath away. I turn out her light, cover her, go to sleep in the living room. To be too near her on the last night would be unbearable. I don't know why. I only know it would be. I lie on the sofa and start the last wait.

I awaken thinking about the first patient I took care of who had multiple sclerosis. She was in tough shape. I came into her room once at five in the morning. I was working nights, making rounds with my flashlight. Everyone was asleep but her. She sat at the edge of the bed, getting dressed—she was being discharged that day. She'd done her bra and panties, and now had rolled her nylons in her hand in preparation for pulling them over her legs. "You're up early," I said, and she smiled and agreed that yes she was. There was the slightest hint of dawn coming through the window, a gray pinkness I could see pushing up over the horizon. It was chilly in there. "Would you like a light on?" I asked, and she said no, that she liked to watch the day come. "Aren't you getting dressed awfully early?" I asked and she said that it took her a very long time. "An hour, start to finish, on a good day," she said. "Today is not a particularly good day."

"Oh," I said, and the tone of my voice revealed a pity I hadn't meant to show.

She looked up at me. "I am going to tell you something now that you will find hard to believe." I waited, listening. "I am happier now than I ever was."

I nodded. "Uh-huh."

"You don't believe me," she said.

"No, I . . . yes, I do."

"No," she said. "You don't. You're so young. When I get home, I'll write you a letter and try to explain it. You're a good nurse, you have real feeling and compassion. The rest will come to you.''

I was embarrassed, and I looked at my watch and pretended I had to leave. Later, I got a seven-page letter in a spidery black script from her, telling me that it took MS to let her see, to let her feel, to let her know she was grounded in her own life. She invited me to a conference for patients with MS. I went with her, listened to a speaker talk about new treatments with steroids. All around me were people in wheelchairs, on crutches, halted in the middle of their lives by an unkind hand on their shoulder. That is what I thought. And yet most of the faces I saw were not bitter. I thought it was only a form of manners, but I was wrong.

Now I lie in Ruth's living room, watching another dawn come, thinking that when you are aware you are dying, the path narrows, and there is room eventually for only one person—you, not distracted by anything else and therefore able to see all that couldn't be seen before. And that this can be such a great gift that you shiver inside at the taking of it.

We are quiet on the way to the airport, all of us busy with the chatter in our own heads, I suppose. Michael is in the back seat, tapping out an occasional riff on his knee. I steal looks at him in the rearview mirror. His eyes are hers, and I am so grateful, suddenly, for the quiet genius of genetics. ''You know, you can always come to our house,'' I always mean to say to him. But I haven't yet. The suitcase he brought is alarmingly small, nothing more than a backpack, really. I wanted to take him aside when I saw it, say, "Go and get a big suitcase. I don't care if it's empty. You carry it anyway."

Ruth stares out the window, impassive; dreamy, even. I sit up straight; keep to the speed limit; remember to signal; wonder, when we hit the highway, if there is any other car the length of this road with passengers so extraordinary. And then realize that of course there is. How is it that we dare to honk at others in traffic, when we know nothing about where they have just come from or what they are on their way to? Ruth used to keep a cardboard sign in her back seat that said, PATIENT, CANCER CARE CENTER. It was so she could park for free in the hospital lot when she went for chemotherapy. But she kept it in her car all the time in case she got stopped for speeding. "When the cop sees it, he'll feel too sorry for me to give me a ticket," she said. "I might as well get some perks from all this." Once she asked me if I'd like her to get me a sign. I said no. Now I wish I'd said yes. I also wish I'd taken one of the morphine pills she used to offer me. All I'd ever done is this: once, while taking a bath, I looked down at my breasts and slapped them.

I drop Michael and Ruth at the door, then go on to the parking lot. It is early afternoon, cold and clear. A good day for flying. Safe. "What if I die while I'm on the plane?" Ruth asked, just before Michael came. "God. How embarrassing. I mean, for him." I slam the car door, consider that when I see it again, she will be gone.

When I come into the terminal, I see L.D. standing beside Ruth. I hadn't known she was coming. Ruth told everyone to stay away, that it would be too hard. I see L.D. embrace Ruth, then turn and walk away. We say nothing as we walk past each other. Her hands are shoved into her pockets. She is dangerous.

"Did you get the tickets?" I ask Michael.

"Didn't have to," Ruth says. She holds up two envelopes. "L.D. traded in the ones she had for Phoenix."

"Really?" At first, I feel a blunt stab of anger, but then the mask drops and I am only afraid. I see now how much L.D. carried hope for all of us, and how much we needed her to do that. I manage a weak, "Oh. Good."

Ruth turns to Michael, asks him to go and get a newspaper from the nearby stand for her to read on the plane. Then, to me, "Let's get this over with, okay? I never have liked good-byes."

"Ruth, do you want me to come with you? I will. I'll go get a ticket right now. We've got plenty of time."

She smiles. "No. Go home, Ann. Hug Meggie. Be nice to Joe. He's not bad, for a man."

"I want to come with you. How can I let you go like this?"

"Here comes Michael," Ruth says, as though it is an answer. And as though I understand and agree with it, I nod. Then I take in a breath, smile, wrap my arms around her, hold her tightly. Her wig smells like her perfume. The dress she has on beneath her tweed coat has a delicate lace collar, and the fabric is black, printed all over with tiny white flowers. I watched her finish

190   making that dress one night when I was at her apartment. She loved the fabric so much, and she put high hopes on what that dress might do for her. She was wearing her half glasses, and she sat hunched over the sewing machine. "You look like a grandma," I told her, and she grunted disapprovingly. The light at the back of the machine hummed, there was a pleasant *thunka-thunk* as the fabric ran under the presser foot of the machine. When she finished the last seam, she snipped at the black thread with her beautiful scissors, then turned the dress right side out to show me how it looked. "And God created the universe," she said. Supposing He did, I thought. He couldn't have felt that much different when He was done.

Ruth is wearing L.D.'s pearl studs, a little make-up—lipstick, some black mascara. She looks only slightly pale. You wouldn't know. "Something to drink?" the stewardess will ask her, bored. Bored!

"Ruth," I say, and start to shake.

"Don't," she whispers.

I kiss her cheek, pull back. "Okay. So call me when you get there."

"Yes."

"Or I'll call you."

"Okay."

"You can call me anytime, you know. The middle of the night. Really, anytime you want. For anything." Tears roll down my face and I brush them away impatiently, as though they are someone else's, as though they are rain.

"I'll call you, Ann. I have to go."

"I know."

Neither of us moves. "Do you need a wheelchair, Mom?" Michael asks, finally. "The gate's a long way down."

"That's a good idea," she says, and when he leaves to get one, she says, "Go now. Pretend this is something normal. And don't think about me on the way home. I don't want you to crack up your car and sue me."

"What would I sue you for?" I ask. "You haven't got shit."

"Oh, boy," she says. "Are you wrong." And now she is crying.

I watch Michael push her away. I have never seen anyone look that way in a wheelchair, sit up so straight and proud. She makes you think it's the only way to get around. She makes you think she's lucky.

I close the car door, put on my seat belt, search the dashboard for the claim ticket. I can smell her, feel her. I look over at the seat she sat in, then out the front windshield. It seems much too wide, and for a moment I think I got in the wrong car. I get out to check the license plate. No. It's the right car. Just the wrong size. When I get home, I'll tell Joe we need a new, smaller car.

I pay the parking lot attendant, an outrageously beautiful young black woman who is playing a radio loudly, tapping her heel against the rung of her high metal stool to the rhythm of someone I've never heard.

192   "Have a nice day," she says, and I say, "You, too." And then, "Why are you doing this? You could be a model."

"Well, thank you."

"Really," I say. "You should call someone. I think there are agencies in the Yellow Pages."

She smiles tightly, looks pointedly past me.

"Oh—sorry," I say, looking into my rearview at the cars lined up behind me.

"It's okay. But if you could just move on, now."

I ride inside the shell that drives my car home, wondering why I said what I did to the parking attendant. I believe it was the need to try to keep saving something.

When I pull into my driveway, I see a plane passing directly overhead. Of course it isn't Ruth. I only make it be, and I watch it until it disappears.

The house is empty. Meg is still at school, Joe at work. The living room looks different from the way I remember it. I feel as though I've been gone for years, and am a stranger here now, vaguely uncomfortable and overly aware of colors and light and the placement of the furniture. I feel as though I'm wearing a kind of bodysuit that keeps me from feeling the real air of home.

I put my suitcase on the stairs to get carried up later, go into the kitchen, open the refrigerator door. Yes, that is the butter we buy. There is some leftover vegetable soup, the ABC kind, Meggie's favorite. I shut the door. The coffeemaker is still on and I turn it off. Joe. He forgets. I look out the window over the kitchen sink for a while, then go to check the answering machine for messages. The light is blinking and I hope it's Ruth, saying, "Oh, all right, you big baby! Come with me." I could still get there. I have time. Or if I miss that flight, I could wait for the next one. But it is not Ruth, it is Helen, saying, "I hope it crashes. I hope one person dies instantly and the rest walk away. Is that a terrible thing to say? Call me."

I go up to my bedroom, pull the shades, get into bed with my shoes on. When Meggie comes home from school, I get up to fix her a snack. "Do you have homework?" I ask, handing her a plate of apple slices.

She nods. I realize that she is acting as though she's afraid of me.

"I'm just sad," I say.

"I know."

"I took Ruth to the airport today. I don't think I'll get to see her again, and so I'm feeling a little sad."

"I know."

"Okay, so I'll just . . . could you just do your homework, Meg?"

"Yes."

"Thank you."

I go back to bed until Joe comes home. I hear the door slam, hear Meg greeting him. "I think we have to go out to dinner again," she says.

He comes into the bedroom, and I feel him sit at the edge of the bed. "Ann?"

I say nothing. I try to, but I can't.

"Can I turn a light on?"

"No."

"Are you . . . do you want to go out to dinner with Meggie and me?"

"No."

"Okay. Well, I'm just going to take her, then."

Silence.

"I'm really hungry," he says.

What is *that*? I want to say. What is "hungry?" What is the matter with you? How can you even say that to me, that you're hungry? But what I say is, "She shouldn't have gone. I can't believe what she stole from us."

Joe sighs. "I know you feel that way. But maybe she only meant to spare you all something."

"No!" I say. "You're just scared. You don't want to deal with it even secondhand. You're glad she's gone because now you can get back to your regular life."

"That's not true. And it's not fair."

"Daddy!" we hear Meggie call. "I'm *hungry!*"

"I'll see you later," Joe says. "I'll bring you something back."

"I don't want anything."

"Maybe you'll change your mind. I'll bring you something back."

He closes the door quietly. I pull the quilt up higher, then cast around inside myself for a moment, looking for symptoms. Then I think, *Oh. That's right. I'm not sick. It's just grief.* I look at my watch. In about half an hour, I can call her. But maybe they got there early. Sometimes there's a good strong tailwind.

Andrew answers on the first ring. "Is Ruth there?" I say, and then, into the questioning silence, "This is her friend, Ann."

"Oh," he says, guardedly friendly. "Of course. Hello, Ann. No, she's not here yet. I was just getting ready to go to the airport. She's actually going to be a little late.''

Late? I think. *Late?* What's the matter with that goddamn airline? She'll be too tired!

"Well," I say. "If you could have her call me when she gets there, all right?''

"I'll tell her.''

"Also, she wanted me to tell you . . . she likes her bed by the window.''

"Yes, I've put it there. She's always liked her bed by the window.''

"Well, I just wanted to make sure.''

"That's fine.''

"She hasn't been eating much.''

"Is that right?''

"No, she doesn't have much of an appetite.''

"I see.''

"She might like some french fries, though. And of course she really likes ice cream.''

He shifts the phone, I can hear the noise of it. And the impatience. Then he says, "Ann, I can't tell you how much I appreciate what you and all your friends have done for Ruth. I want you to know I'll take very good care of her. We've always been very close.''

Huh! I want to say. You're not so close! She used to be very mean to you, I happen to know. When you were little and sleeping in the bunk below her, she told you that ghosts were in the room and she made *whoooo* noises until you cried. She told you the story of the Crucifixion and embellished all the gory details until you cried about that, too. She pretended to turn into another person so you'd say things about her and then

196   she beat you up for what you said. What an idiot you
were, Andrew! And now you object to Ruth's language.
You flinch every time she swears, get a white ring
around your lips, yes, she told me that.

"I know you're close," I say.

"I'll have her call you."

"Thank you."

I go into the bathroom, look at myself. In the mirror, I see Ruth holding her spoon over her cereal that
morning. Her hand was shaking, a fine tremor, and I
was thinking, brain involvement, oh, Jesus, it's her
brain, she's getting worse, please don't let her have a
seizure on the way to the airport. I put my hand on the
mirror, drag it down the surface, note with a sense of
terrible satisfaction the dirty tracks I leave behind.

———— ❧ ————

B y ten o'clock, she still hasn't called me. And I
don't call her. I'll wait until tomorrow, I think. I
sit at the kitchen table in my pajamas eating the
eggplant sub Joe brought me and thinking about a time
before Ruth got sick when we talked about how we
wanted to die. "I think I want a massive heart attack," I
said. "Sudden death. But no matter what gets me, I
want the last thing in the world I feel to be peace."

"Not me," she'd said. "The last thing I want to
feel is . . . dazzled."

"That's a pretty tall order," I'd said, and she'd
said, "Yes. But it's what I want."

How will she get that now, I wonder. How?

W hen I climb into bed beside him, Joe turns on his side and reaches out toward me. I think, if he tries to get laid I will kill him with a butcher knife. And then I start to cry because he is only Joe, touching my hair, pushing it back from my face because he knows I love it when he does that, and that is all, it is whitely innocent.

"Who knows why people make the decisions they do?" he says softly. "Especially when they're dying. Maybe this was just something she couldn't explain. Maybe it had nothing to do with you."

Maybe it didn't, I think. The pull of family is formidable, I know. I haven't yet let myself feel how grateful I am to be back in my own bed, but I know it's coming. And I know I'd better get ready. Because feeling good will feel awful.

I got my hair cut," I tell Ruth, a couple of days later.

"Really? What's it look like?"

"It looks like hell," I say. "I told him an inch and he heard 'Shave it.' "

"Beauty seclusion again?"

"Are you kidding? I put on a scarf to go to the bathroom."

The inevitable pause. "So," I say. "How are you?"

"You know," she says, "I was thinking today about how I used to get so pissed off just because my laundry hamper was full. Now it takes so little to make me happy. This is good to finally learn, you know what I mean? It's not so bad, Ann, honest. It's kind of interesting. I sort of feel like I'm only going home, like I'm being called in first, like when we were kids. Of course we always hated to go, right?—everybody *else* got to stay out, there was still some *light,* but then when you got in, you were sort of glad to be there. I think I'll be glad to be there. I just don't want to be in pain, so I've got lots of stuff around in case I need it."

I look out the window. "Do you look the same?"

"I don't know. I don't look in the mirror anymore. It's getting pretty messy, Ann. You're not missing a thing."

"Yes, I am."

"Do you look the same?" she asks.

"Yeah, except for my marine haircut. And I've gained even more weight. I guess I *don't* look the same."

I can hear her smile. Then she asks, "Did you see the full moon last night?"

"Yes! So big!"

"Yes."

And then we don't talk for a while. I think we are both savoring the fact that there is still something we can see at the same time. Ruth once said that the best parameters of her mental health were her skin and her awareness of what phase the moon was in.

"Ann?" she says. "I'm kind of whipped, okay?"

That's how she always ends the conversations.

———e———

I read a good book," I tell her. "Want me to send it?"

"I don't think so." She sounds so tired today.

"I made this new recipe last night," I say. "You use a whole bunch of mustard on chicken. It sounds terrible, but it's really good."

"Have you seen Helen?" she asks. "L.D.?"

"No. But I will."

"Promise me, okay?"

"I promise."

———e———

Our conversations are silly—about nothing, really, less and less consequential. But they are comforting to both of us, I know. They remind me of what we talk about before we go to sleep, any of us, the lazy, low-voiced assurances we offer each other: *Did you turn out the lights? Put the chain locks on? Is the cat in? Are the kids covered?* Always, we're just checking to see that we're safe. I've always thought that was the funniest thing, given the vastness of the dark we lie down in.

After two more days, she can't come to the phone anymore. Talking takes too much energy, too much breath. I talk to Andrew instead. I make brief, awkward inquiries, and he offers brief, awkward responses. Helen says she hates him, he won't tell her anything, but there is nothing to say. "Should we go there?" we all ask each other, in our different combinations. I don't know, I don't know, we all say. And we wait. I make brownies, look up from the mixer, burst into tears, wipe my face with my apron, and finish. "Hello?" I say, too anxiously, every time the phone rings.

Would you please buy her a bouquet for me?" I ask Andrew. "I'll send you a check. But I want you to go pick it out yourself to make sure the flowers are good. She'll have a fit if they're not good flowers."

"To tell you the truth," he says. "She's not really too interested in anything now."

"All purples and pinks and whites," I say. "No carnations. A really big one. Plenty of freesia, so it smells good."

"Ann, you'd really be wasting your money."

"She always likes to have fresh flowers. She needs them."

"All right. When the nurse comes today, I'll go get her some. How much do you want me to spend?"

"What does the nurse come for?" I ask.

"Oh, just . . . She bathes her, helps with medication, with the oxygen."

"She's using oxygen?"

"Yes, it's been pretty hard for her to breathe. Especially at night, for some reason."

I remember her doctor saying, "It will most likely be respiratory, Ruth. A lot of people like to go into the hospital at that point because the feeling of not being able to breathe . . . well. Anyway, at the hospital we can give you enough medication to make you comfortable."

Ruth said, "You mean you can kill me that way, instead," and her doctor said, well yes, that was one way to look at it.

She looked at me then, popped her bubble gum, raised her eyebrows up and down. And when we got in my car outside, she said, " 'A lot of people *like to go to the hospital.*' Did you hear that?"

"Yeah. I thought that was a pretty poor choice of words myself."

"Well, I guess so," she said. "You know how I felt, hearing him say that?"

"How?"

"Look," she said, and when I did, she slowly pulled her wig up off her head, saying, "Eeeeeyikes!"

"Put some baby orchids in that bouquet, too," I tell Andrew now.

202   "All right. And you wanted to spend . . ."

"I'm sending you a check for a hundred dollars."

"That's way too much!"

"Find a way to spend it," I tell him. "Use long stems."

Michael comes home, goes to stay with his dad. Ruth's request. It must be getting very close. "Is she scared?" I ask Andrew.

"I don't think so," he says.

"You haven't asked her?"

"No."

"Well, Jesus, Andrew, go ask her, and then come back to the phone and tell me what she said."

He puts the phone down, and I hear him saying my name and then some other things. Then he comes back to the phone. "She wrote no. Then she wrote that she loves you."

"Thank you," I say, and hang up.

She "wrote." What else will be taken from her before she leaves?

I go to the grocery store. I go to the post office. I fold the towels, stack them in the linen closet. I sit on the edge of the bathtub and weep, and then I clean it with Soft Scrub.

---⊛---

Tell her that I will always talk to her. Remind her."

"She's pretty much sleeping all the time now, Ann."

"Tell her when she's sleeping."

---⊛---

I open the mail. I roll the socks up, put them away. I read articles in magazines. I watch *Seinfeld* and *Nightline* with Joe. I've begun taking antacids for the regular grabbing pain in my stomach.

---⊛---

I have lunch with Helen, and she tells me about the time she and Ruth had to dissect a fetal pig together in biology class. "We got in trouble that day because the teacher heard us talking about butt-fucking. We couldn't help it. We'd just heard about it, and we couldn't believe it. We had to talk about it. But then we got kicked out of class and Ruth was really pissed because she'd wanted to cut the pig's heart out that day and send it to her boyfriend, Chuckie Lokenwitz."

"What'd she want to do that for?"

Helen shrugs. "It was Valentine's Day."

204   We laugh, and for a moment it's like when we were all at her house. But then it is just the two of us again, without her, and it's different. I am reminded of public television specials that demonstrate the importance of everything needing to be on the right spot on the right chain, or things turn out to be something else, something wrong.

J oe and I are going out to dinner so I am making Meg Kraft macaroni and cheese even though I worry about the yellow dye. He called from work a while ago, suggested I try to get a last-minute sitter, that he'd call back in a few minutes to see if I could. If so, he'll go to the restaurant right from work, meet me there. When the phone rings, I pick it up and say, ''Good news!''

''. . . Hello?'' I hear a voice say.

''Andrew?''

''Yes.''

He never calls me. I know why he's calling now. I start crying and some part of me held in permanent abeyance says, well, would you look at that. Look how fast those tears come. As if they're always on the ready. Which of course they are.

''What time?'' I ask Andrew.

He sighs. ''Three thirty-seven this morning.''

''Thank you,'' I say, and hang up. Then I pick up the receiver again, get halfway through dialing before I realize who I am calling: Ruth, to tell her she died.

I tear a piece of paper from the newspaper lying on the kitchen table, write down the date and 3:37 A.M., put it in my apron pocket. Then I push a dishtowel up to my mouth. The sounds I make remind me of those I heard coming from myself when I was in labor.

Meggie comes down from her room, silently crosses the kitchen and puts her arms around me. I spread my hand flat and hard against her back to feel the movement of air into, then out of her; then back into her again. I subtract nine years from forty-four.

———— ❧ ————

T hat night, at my request, Joe takes Meggie to a movie. I walk around the house, touching things: a book, the smooth surface of the kitchen counter, Meggie's bear that smells like her. Then I get into the bathtub, lie back with a wet washrag over my face, and let go. It is a howling, really, a self-indulgent letting go of some part of my awful pain. And then, I sense her presence. I sit up, pull the washrag off my face, frightened and exhilarated. She will appear, see-through, say something so wise and healing I can easily go on. But she does not appear. I only hear her voice inside my head. "Knock it off," she says. And I do.

Meggie wants to come to the funeral and she wants to wear black. She has a black skirt and black leotards and a black sweatshirt and that is what she wears, though with her school's name turned to the inside. She sits in a church pew beside Joe. Two rows behind them I see Joel Fratto, his hands folded in his lap. His face is remarkably impassive; only his hands speak.

I sit in the front row with Helen, L.D., and Sarah. Sarah wears a beautiful green dress, Helen a forties special that Ruth loved: a brown print dress with huge buttons, a matching veiled hat. I wear a red miniskirt, which is what she told me to do. L.D. is wearing a black, ill-fitting suit belonging to her mother, who apparently is just about the same impressive size. She is wearing nylons that smash the hairs on her legs into a pattern you might find on a sofa, and she has on low black patent-leather heels. Heels! We don't any of us know what to say and anyway, L.D.'s face told us not to try. We all read something we've written about Ruth, and though I have an awareness of people standing and saying things, myself included, I don't know what they are. I can't stop crying and finally I stop trying to. Tears seem beside the point, something like my hair color. I can't retain what anyone is saying to me, but everyone keeps talking. I feel as though I'm in a field of bees.

After the church service, the four of us drive in Sarah's car to the nearby cemetery. There they are, the same two trees Ruth showed Michael and me, the stream that now you can hear running. Helen pulls me aside, wipes at my face. "Stop crying," she says tenderly, and then starts herself.

"I wish she'd have let us see her," Helen says.

"I know."

"I guess she thought we shouldn't see her looking so bad."

"Do you think that was Ruth who decided that?" I ask. "Or Andrew? Doesn't seem like Ruth. Seems like if it was Ruth worrying about looking bad, she'd have the funeral guy put a mask on her."

"I know. Nixon or something."

"Maybe we should ask Andrew to let us see her before they lower it in."

"L.D. already asked. He told her no."

"Really!" I say, with some admiration.

Someone turns around to hush us up, there is a little speech being given by the minister. And then people begin walking away. Wait, I think. Is this it? Is this all? I'm not ready to leave her. I see Joe and Meggie put flowers on the casket and walk away. There are so many flowers. She would have loved it. Eventually, I am the only one left. But then I hear the sounds of someone quietly weeping. I walk around to the other side of the casket and see L.D. sitting on the ground, her face

208 shoved into her hands, her legs splayed out before her. "L.D.?" I say softly.

She looks up. "I never even told her my name. I wanted her to keep on wanting to know, to have some questions that needed answering, so she'd stay alive." She is not wearing a coat, and she starts shivering violently. "As if that would keep her alive! I never told her what my name is, and she really wanted to know."

"Well . . . What is it?" I ask. "Tell me."

She looks up at me with her huge, tortured face. "It's Lolly fucking Dawn," she says. "Okay?"

"Yes," I say. "Okay." I squat down, put my arms around her. She is so cold. Her hands, holding on to each other, are reddened and chapped already. "We have to go, L.D.," I say. "She's not here."

I like to think that she looked out the window one last time the night she died, and saw with a new understanding the placement of the stars. I like to think something incomprehensibly vast and complex moved into her soul at that moment, and that it, not pathology, was what took her breath away.

I go bowling with L.D. and Sarah and Helen every other Wednesday night. We had shirts made up: Big Balls Bowling League on the back, our names in script over our pockets in the front. Once we got kicked out for L.D. starting a fight with the people who were bowling next to us and took exception to the fact that my gutter balls were crossing over into their lane. The other times, it's just normal fun: beer, potato chips, good talking, a lot of hard laughter. Sometimes my stomach hurts the next day from it.

I go to the cemetery about twice a week. It's a pretty place. And Ruth's grave always has something new on it: a carved loon, seashells, vases filled with field flowers, beautiful rocks and feathers. Once when I came, a Gumby was leaning insolently against her headstone. And another time there were thin white ribbons hanging from one of the two trees, and a tiny angel on a string with her face fixed upward. Helen planted bulbs around the headstone that will bloom every spring.

And of course I do still talk to her. I make a ceremony of it: lie down, close my eyes, open myself beyond opening in an effort to reach her, and to receive her. Then I start telling her things, out loud. But I never feel anything back. This pisses me off. We had a deal. To test the equipment, I ask to feel my life force. I've been doing this since I was ten years old, and every time I ask for it, it comes to me: I feel a hard thrill of acknowledgment pass wide through the length of me. I

210 believe I am effectively unconscious at that moment, in a holy place between me and the Mystery. This phenomenon is beyond normality, beyond the usual understanding, I know. So when I feel it I know everything is ready for her to come. But she doesn't. Still, I keep trying. As I promised. I am trying so hard to do everything I promised. Even when I go to sleep. These days it's always on the side of the bed by the open window, with the drapes pulled out of the way. It's not so I can watch the stars, as she did. It's in case a breeze comes by. It's so she can find me.

•This year, breast cancer will be newly diagnosed every three minutes, and a woman will die from breast cancer every 12 minutes.

•Breast cancer is the leading cause of cancer death for African-American women.

•Five percent of the money spent for cancer research is spent on breast cancer.

Statistics from the Women's Action Coalition's booklet *The Facts About Women.*

You can help with breast-cancer research by calling The National Breast Cancer Coalition, 1-800-935-0434, or writing them at P.O. Box 66373, Washington, D.C. 20035.

This book was set in Perpetua, a typeface designed by the English artist Eric Gill, and cut by The Monotype Corporation between 1928 and 1930. Perpetua is a contemporary face of original design, without any direct historical antecedents. The shapes of the roman letters are derived from the techniques of stonecutting. The larger display sizes are extremely elegant and form a most distinguished series of inscriptional letters.